REDWOOD PIONEER
BETTY STIRLING

Cover design by Elle Staples
Cover illustration by Tanya Glebova
Illustrations by Ursula Koering
This unabridged version has updated grammar and spelling.
First published in 1955
© 2019 Jenny Phillips
www.thegoodandthebeautiful.com

Table of Contents

1. Goodbye, Potato Farm 1
2. Santa Cruz 9
3. Road to the Redwoods 16
4. Friend for a Day 24
5. A Midnight Visitor 28
6. Timber! 35
7. Tree-Splitting 43
8. Mountain Garden 49
9. A Cabin at Last 57
10. Crawdad 61
11. Exploring Pie Creek 69
12. The Little Irish Rose 80
13. Mike's Caterpillar 85
14. The Stranger 91
15. Mike in Charge 104
16. Grizzly! 110

Chapter 1
Goodbye, Potato Farm

Mike O'Grady was moving from the little valley where he had lived all his life. He turned and took one long last look at the cabin. It seemed so forlorn and lonesome sitting there in the middle of the unplowed potato fields.

He rubbed first one blue eye and then the other. But he was not going to cry, even if he did feel as lonesome as the little cabin looked. Mike was going to be a pioneer, and pioneers are brave.

"Mike, come on, quickly!" called his sister Martha.

Mike turned and ran after the slow-moving wagon. Bossy and Maury, the two sleek cows, switched their tails at him as he caught up. They were tied to the back of the wagon. Mike skipped past the cows. Sean and Liam, his two little brothers, and Mary, his little sister, were sitting in the back of the wagon. Their bare feet swung over the end, and they giggled when Mike tickled them with an oat straw.

Mike ran ahead of the two donkeys and caught up with Pat and Tom, his older brothers. They were walking ahead with the third donkey, who was loaded with the odds and ends that wouldn't fit into the wagon. Pat and Tom were talking about mysterious big-boy things and didn't even notice Mike as he trudged along beside them.

He wished he weren't the middle one of the family. There was no one his size to talk to. Tom and Mary were the nearest to his age, but Tom was five years older and Mary was four years younger. Martha was only a little older than Tom, but she didn't count anyway. She was always busy. Why, she was almost a second ma to the little ones. The big boys had all the fun, too. They always went places with Pa. Mike, the middle one, had to stay home with the younger children.

Mike pulled a couple of green oat stalks to chew on. If Pat and Tom wouldn't talk to him, he would walk with his father.

They came to the top of the hill that separated their old home from the sight of any other cabins. From here they could look down on a valley that was dotted with small potato farms, and beyond that, there were more green hills.

"I see two more cabins, Pa," Mike said as they started down the narrow road. He often came to this hill to hunt rabbits for dinner, and he watched for new cabins.

"Too many people, Mike, too many people." Patrick O'Grady shook his head.

Mike looked up at his pa. There were no neighbors near their old cabin yet.

"When you were born, Mike," his father went on, "all of this valley was wild. There wasn't a single cabin. Not a one. In less than ten years, all these cabins and houses have been built. In another year or two, the whole valley will be cleared and planted."

He pulled on the reins. One of the donkeys was trying to eat the grass at the side of the road. "Giddap, lazy one," he said.

The donkeys plodded on slowly. The road went downhill, but not steeply. The wagon couldn't roll fast on its big wooden wheels. Mike jerked up another couple of oat straws to chew. He liked to draw them through the place in the side of his mouth where he had pulled out a baby tooth last week. He rubbed the straw over the sharp edge of the new tooth.

"By next year there will be other cabins near our old cabin, Mike," his father said again. "That's too close. We need room to stretch. So it's off to the wilderness again for us." He looked pleased.

Mike sighed. He almost wished that he didn't have so much room to stretch. He wanted someone to play with.

They were passing the first farm now. Three small children stood wide-eyed at the side of the road to watch. Mike tried to look grown up as he walked past them, but he peeked out of the corners of his eyes.

The biggest of the little girls said, "Hello," shyly.

Mike smiled at her. "Hello," he said, and walked right on. He wasn't used to strange children. He didn't know what else to say.

By dinnertime they had come to the top of the green hills they had seen beyond the valley. Mike had never been this far from home before.

While his mother and Martha spread out a cloth under a big oak tree and set out the cold food, Mike stood still and stared at the country ahead. He had never seen such a big valley before. So many, many farms! Such big houses!

But the thing that he stared at the most was the faraway blue ocean. All his life he had wanted to see the ocean.

Pat and Tom had been to Santa Cruz before with Pa. They had bragged about how they had seen the ocean. They had even walked on the sand and waded in the water. Mike did hope that he would be able to walk on the beach. But he was a wee bit afraid. Pat had said that the ocean roared and that the waves sprayed high.

Mary ran to him. "Isn't it big, Mike? I didn't know the whole world was so big," she chattered.

"There are as many houses as stars in the sky at night," said Mike.

"Come and eat," said Ma.

Mike forgot the ocean, the valley, and the houses. He was hungry. It had been a long time since breakfast. He began gobbling a thick slice of bread covered with sweet butter. Then he saw little Liam copying him. Liam was almost choking on the big bites.

Mike suddenly remembered all that Ma had said about taking little bites and chewing with the mouth closed. When he started taking little bites, Liam copied him and didn't choke anymore. His mother noticed and smiled at him.

Dinner was soon over and the donkeys hitched to the wagon again.

"On to Santa Cruz!" shouted Pat, clapping his hands over his head.

"Santa Cruz by dark!" yelled Tom.

"Will we really get to Santa Cruz by tonight?" Mike asked his father. His eyes were shining. He had never been in a city in his whole life.

"That's right!" said Pa. "Here we go!"

The road was wider now. They were partway down the hill when they met another wagon, pulled by horses. A boy the size of Mike was sitting on the high front seat with a man. He grinned down at Mike.

"Going to Santa Cruz?" he asked.

"Yes," said Mike. "Have you been there?"

"Oh, sure," said the boy. "Lots of times."

Mike felt more timid than ever. He wondered if he were the only boy his size who had never been to the city. They passed many farms now. There were orchards just beginning to bloom. There were green waving grain fields, and there were potato fields, newly planted.

Mike was so excited that he wanted to run. Wouldn't they ever get to Santa Cruz?

They passed a big house with a tower on top and a bell in the tower. In front of the house was a pole with the United States flag. He counted the thirteen red and white stripes and the thirty-seven stars when the wind flapped it out.

"What is that house, Pa?" he asked.

"A school, Mike. Boys and girls go there to learn to read and write."

"I can read and write," said Mike. "And I never went to a school to learn."

"You have a smart mother, Mike," his father said. "You are lucky that she has taught you to read and write. But maybe you'll have a chance to go to school someday, maybe to college. Who knows?"

"A college? What's that?" Mike asked.

"A school for boys bigger than Pat, even. They go to college to learn to be teachers and preachers and doctors," said Pa. "Last time I was here in Santa Cruz, I heard tell of a new college being built in San Jose. San Jose's only a day or so by coach over the mountains. Maybe you can go to college there someday, Mike."

Mike couldn't talk anymore. He hadn't known there were so many things in the world. He watched the sun getting lower over the bright blue ocean. He could feel the sea breeze now. It wasn't like the warm breeze in the little valleys. But it smelled like the fog that rolled in to cover the hills and valleys almost every night in the winter and spring.

Suddenly Mike heard a terrifying noise. It was like thunder and screeching and wind all rolled together. He covered his ears and got close to his father. His little brothers and sister cried in terror.

"What is it, Pa?" he cried. "What is it?"

Pa was laughing. "It's a train, Mike. I've told you about trains. Look!"

Mike cautiously uncovered his ears. He looked across a field toward the west. A monster was puffing along, spouting black smoke and sparks from a chimney in the top. It was pulling wagons, and one wagon was something like a long cabin with windows along the sides.

Mike stared and stared until the train was out of sight over the little hill. He had really seen a train. What a wonderful trip this was!

Soon they came to the top of the hill the train had gone over. Ahead of them, toward the setting sun, Mike could see more houses. Big houses and little houses—more houses than he had known were in the whole world. He couldn't even count them.

"Santa Cruz!" shouted Pat. "We're almost there!"

Mike felt tired, but he was too excited to care. In just a little while, he would be in Santa Cruz.

Chapter 2

Santa Cruz

Mike walked beside the wagon as the tired donkeys pulled it down the main street of Santa Cruz. The sun had set, and the sky was getting dark. A man was lighting little fires on posts along the street.

"What is he doing?" Mike asked.

"Lighting the street lights," said Pa. "There's gas in little pipes inside the posts. When he lights the gas, it will keep burning until he shuts the gas off."

They trudged along. Mike turned his head this way and that, trying to see everything. The street was hard and smooth, not dusty or muddy or full of ruts like the country roads.

His father saw him scuffing the road, trying to see why it was so smooth. "It's paved, Mike," Pa said. "They cut oily rock and lay it on the ground. Makes a road that never gets muddy."

Pa led them to the edge of the town, and they found a grassy field where they could camp. Pat and Tom put up the tent. Mike was so tired he could hardly move, but he hunted under a tree in the dark for some sticks for the fire.

Soon Pa had the fire going. He put a log on it that he had carried in the wagon. Ma put a kettle over the fire and began to cook the stew. Martha made beds in the tent, and

Mary helped her. Everyone was busy but Sean and Liam. They were fast asleep in the back of the wagon.

Pa looked across the fire at Mike. "Mike," he said, "do you want to sleep inside the tent with Ma and Martha and the little ones? Or do you want to sleep outside with Pat and Tom and me?"

Mike shivered. He had never slept outdoors. But he did want to be a big boy like Pat and Tom. He stood as high as Ma's chin now.

"I'll—I'll sleep outside," he said.

Pa nodded. "Good boy," he said.

After supper, Mike rolled up in his quilts between Pa and Tom. He pulled the covers almost over his head. Then he peeked out to see the stars. One by one they were being hidden by the fog blowing in from the ocean. Soon all was

quiet, and Mike could hear the small sound of the ocean, going up and down, seeming far away like a dream.

The next thing he knew, the sun was peeking through the fog, and he could smell the breakfast Ma was frying over the fire. He jumped up.

After breakfast, they staked out the donkeys in the field. Then they all walked into town. It looked even more wonderful to Mike than it had the night before.

There were flower gardens in almost all the front yards, and some of the paths were bordered with shells. Mike had seen some shells before, when Pat and Tom brought them home from Santa Cruz. Mike hoped he would be able to get some shells at the ocean to keep for his very own.

Soon they came to the stores. Pa went into a big store that smelled of sawdust, leather, and paint. Pa went in first, and then Pat and Tom and Martha and Mike and Mary and Sean, and then Ma and Liam, who was holding tightly to Ma's hand.

The storekeeper laughed. "Quite a family you got there, man," he said to Pa. "And they all look like Irishmen, every last one of them."

"Sure, and every last one of them is an Irishman," said Pa.

Then they all laughed.

The storekeeper gave each one of them a piece of sugar candy. Mike turned his over and over, but he finally popped it into his mouth. Only once before had he ever had a piece of store candy.

"What can I do for you today?" the storekeeper was saying.

Pa looked at a long list in his hand. "I'll need nails—about a keg of them, all sizes. Put in lots of big ones."

Mike watched the storekeeper measure out the different sizes of square nails.

"Going to build a house?" the storekeeper asked.

"Yes," said Pa.

"Around here?"

"No," Pa said. "We're heading for the redwoods. It's getting too crowded here for me."

"Lots of new folks here, all right," said the storekeeper. "Last I heard, they said Santa Cruz County had over eight thousand people. So you're off for the big timber—farming or logging?"

"Neither," said Pa. "I'll be cutting tanbark for the tanneries. Good money in it, they say."

Mike wandered around the store, looking at the tools, plows, kegs of nails, and harnesses. Finally he went back to the counter. The man tied all of Pa's purchases into a big bundle, and then Pa paid him.

"We'll get some new clothes," said Pa, as they all filed out to the street again.

Mike went toward the middle of the street.

"Mike, come back," said Pat. "You walk on this part close to the buildings. It's called the sidewalk. The street is only for the horses and wagons."

Mike scurried back to the sidewalk just as a fancy carriage pulled by two glistening horses raced down the street.

They went into a dry goods store. Mike's eyes opened wide when he saw the shelves and shelves of bolts of cloth, shoes, shirts, and many other things. He walked all around, with his hands behind his back.

Suddenly he heard Pa call him. "Come here, Mike, you are to have a pair of shoes."

Mike sat still while the storekeeper measured his feet and found a pair of shoes his size. Then he got a new shirt, a new pair of pants, and a jacket. It was the first store-bought shirt he had had. This was almost like Christmas, even if it was only early May.

After Pa had bought everything on the list, he sent Pat after the wagon. They took everything back to the tent, and then they ate dinner.

After dinner, they walked back to town. This was the part of the day Mike was looking forward to. They were going to the beach.

Little Liam had had too much excitement in the morning. His feet began to stumble and his eyes to droop. Soon Pa held the little lad against his shoulder, and Liam was fast asleep.

Mike began to run when they could see the waves. He wriggled his bare toes in the sand and stared at the waves chasing each other up on the beach.

"Help us build a castle, Mike," said Pat.

The three boys set to work building in the sand. Mike thought this was great fun. Soon they had the castle finished, and he ran along the beach picking up shells.

"Don't be a pig, Mike," said Martha, when she saw his pockets bulging.

"There will be as many again tomorrow," said Pa. "The ocean washes them up every night."

Mike spread them out in a row. Some were big and others were tiny.

"Choose the best ones to keep," said Pa. "You won't be able to carry many."

Mike tried to choose the best ones, but that was hard. He still had his pockets full after he had sorted them. The younger children had their pockets full, too. Pat had only one shell, but it was a beauty. Pat said it was a sand dollar, and that it brought good luck.

"I hope so," said Ma. "We'll need all the good luck we can get before we are settled again."

"That's right," said Pa. "And we'd better be getting back to the tent now for supper—"

"'Cause tomorrow we head for the redwoods," sang Mike, dancing a jig in the sand. "We'll be redwood pioneers!"

Chapter 3

Road to the Redwoods

Mike rubbed his eyes sleepily. Surely it wasn't time to get up. But Pa was shaking him.

"Get up, Mike," Pa said. "We have a long way to go today."

Mike scrambled out of the warm covers. "To the redwoods, to the redwoods," he said to himself as he buttoned his shirt.

He grabbed the milk pail and began milking Bossy. Tom was already milking Maury, and Pat was starting the fire. The sun hadn't yet come through the fog over the mountains, so Mike knew it was early.

Breakfast was over quickly, and then Mr. O'Grady roped down the load on the wagon. He tied the chicken crate on top, and Mike covered most of the crate with an old cloth so that the chickens wouldn't be frightened at strange sights and noises. Mary and Sean and Liam climbed onto the back of the wagon, and Pa shook the reins.

"Giddap," he said. "We're off!"

Mike walked ahead of the wagon. Even if Tom and Pat wouldn't talk to him much, he wanted to be out in front to see everything first. He had seen many redwood trees before. He had even seen the big redwood forest, but only from far away. But today he was going into the real forest where the big trees were. Pa had said that the redwood trees were the tallest trees on the whole earth.

The road followed the San Lorenzo River. Mike picked up a handful of pebbles to throw into the water as he walked. A barge loaded with lumber floated down the river. Mike waved to the men on the deck, and they waved back.

They passed a group of sprawling, reddish-colored buildings. Mike tried to spell out the name painted on the biggest building.

"It's the tannery, Mike," said Pa. "That's where we'll be bringing the bark this fall."

Mike was glad they didn't stop at the tannery. He didn't like the smell.

There were wildflowers in bloom along the roadsides. Mike knew the poppies and the lupines, but there were other flowers that he didn't know. He picked a bouquet for Mary.

Mike could see men working on the other side of the road from the river. Some had picks, others had shovels, and some were pounding with heavy sledgehammers.

"What are they doing, Pa?" he asked.

Pa shook his head. "I don't know, Mike."

Then they came to a place where the river valley was suddenly narrow. Here the men were beginning to dig a tunnel through the hill. Mike did wish he could find out why they were digging, but he was too timid to ask.

Pat stared at the workers. "What are you building?" he called.

One of the men straightened up and wiped his face. "A railroad," he said.

"Where to?" asked Pat.

"Santa Cruz to San Jose, through Felton," said the man. He picked up the sledgehammer and began to pound again.

Pa was driving the wagon right on, but Mike ran over to watch the railroad builders laying the narrow track on the crossties. Then he had to hurry to catch up with the family. He wished they could go more slowly. He wanted to see everything.

Soon they were entering the edge of the redwood forest. Mike was thrilled. The road wound between trees so tall that he could hardly see the tops. Some were so big around that he was sure Pat and Tom and Pa together wouldn't be nearly able to reach around them.

Once Mike saw a deer peeking through some brush. "Where's my gun?" asked Pat.

Mike was glad to see Pa shake his head and say, "No shooting now, Pat." The deer had looked so pretty standing there watching them.

Mike was feeling hollow inside by the time the sun was overhead. "When do we eat?" he asked Pa.

"We'll stop in Felton," said Pa. "It can't be much farther now."

Mike could see nothing but trees. He wondered if there really could be a town hidden somewhere along this road. He was afraid he would starve before they ever got there.

They came over a little hill.

"I see houses ahead," said Pat.

Mike strained his eyes. He couldn't see any houses. Maybe if he were as tall as Pat— Then the donkey with the load gave a loud "hee-haw." She must have heard another donkey, Mike thought. Maybe if he had ears as big as hers, he could hear another donkey, too. He tightened his belt. It wouldn't be long till dinner now.

When they finally reached Felton, Mike wasn't much impressed with it. He had been to Santa Cruz. He returned the stares of the children who stood at the side of the road and watched them pass.

The biggest thing in Felton was a huge house with many porches. It was even bigger than the houses in Santa Cruz. Mike asked Pa about it.

"It's a hotel," said Pa. "Rich people come here in the summertime to be lazy."

Mike laughed. He thought Pa was joking. Surely people couldn't go some place just to be lazy. Grownups had to work. But he took a second look at the big building.

They stopped for dinner at the edge of the little town. Mike took the two cows down to the edge of the river to drink, and Tom led the donkeys. Then Mike climbed up on the wagon and gave the chickens a pan of water in their crate. They clucked and drank greedily.

Mike patted his stomach as they started on again. He felt much better now that it was full again.

All afternoon they plodded up the narrow road. Mike could see nothing but trees and the blue sky overhead, and sometimes the river beside them or a little ways off. He felt as if he were shut in a crate like the chickens.

Pa knew the names of the trees. He told Mike which were madrones, with the shiny red-brown bark, which were nutmegs, and which were azaleas. A few times he pointed out tanbark oaks. Mike watched for these especially. But mostly he saw redwoods; huge, tall redwoods and more redwoods everywhere.

Pa was trying to hurry. He wanted to reach Boulder before dark. Mike didn't see how they could go any faster, though he shivered when he thought about having to stay along the road in the forest during the night. The forest was too wet to camp in, Mike thought. There were moss and ferns everywhere, and little yellow violets.

"Why is everything so wet, Pa?" he asked.

"Lots of rain here," said Pa. "I heard someone say in Santa Cruz that they have 90 inches of rain up here at Boulder."

"Why, Pa!" exclaimed Pat. "Did they say 90 inches?"
Pa nodded his head. "That's what they said."
"But, Pa," Pat protested, "that's seven and a half feet!"
"That's right," agreed Pa. "That's why the redwoods grow so tall."

Mike whistled. Why, that was taller than a big man. Wouldn't that make a real lake if it all piled up at once?

The sun disappeared early, hidden by the mountains that rose on each side of the river. Mike's legs were tired, and he was cold. He found his new jacket in the back of the wagon and buttoned it up to his neck. He wondered if they would ever get to Boulder.

Once in a while Mike could catch a glimpse of a large wooden trough built near the road. He could hear water

running in it, and he wondered what it was for. Finally Tom climbed up to see.

"It's a flume," Tom reported. "There's lumber floating down in it."

Mike scrambled up to see, with Tom's help. The flume was about four feet across and was made of closely fitted planks two inches thick. Mike guessed it was three or four feet deep. He wondered where the lumber floating in it came from and where it went.

Pa said it must come from Boulder, because he had been told that Boulder was only a sawmill and a few houses for the sawmill workers. But he didn't know where it went.

"Maybe to Felton," he said. "Maybe they put the lumber on wagons or river barges there. I don't know."

They plodded on. Everyone was too tired to talk. Mary, Sean, and Liam were asleep in the back of the wagon. Mike almost wished he were little, too, so that he could climb up there and sleep awhile.

It was getting dark when they finally saw the lights of Boulder shining through the trees. There were no gas street lights here, but only little kerosene lamps in the windows.

Dogs barked as they stopped on the short street. A man came out and Pa talked to him. The man showed them where they could camp for the night, and his wife hurried out with a kettle of soup.

"You must be cold," she said.

"We'll soon warm up," said Pa, kindling a fire.

"There's good water from the spring," said the woman. "Help yourself." She smiled when she saw the sleeping little ones in the wagon when the firelight shone on their faces. "So long a trip," she said. "Little fellows get tired."

Mike was so tired when he crawled down into his blankets that he could hardly remember that they had come to the end of the road. In another day they would go into the redwood forest.

Chapter 4

Friend for a Day

The sun was shining when Mike woke up, and Boulder was noisy with the day's work. Mike sat up slowly. Pa had let him sleep late.

"Good morning, sleepyhead," said Ma. She patted his tousled hair as she handed him a plate of breakfast.

Mike peeked into the tent. Mary, Sean, and Liam were still asleep. He saw that Martha was milking for him, so he sat down on a rock and ate his food.

Soon Pa, Pat, and Tom returned.

"It's all settled," said Pa. "We can leave the wagon at the Haddens' house, and also whatever we can't pack into the forest by donkey. I can come back with the donkeys after the cabin is built and get the rest of the load."

"Will we start today?" Mike asked eagerly. Now that he had come this far, he was anxious to be a real pioneer.

"No," said Pa. "We'll need most of the day to get the loads repacked so's we can leave early tomorrow. Pat, Tom, Ma, and I will be busy this morning. Martha will have to look after the little ones. So—I reckon you might as well look over the town."

Mike was delighted. There wasn't much to see in the town, though. But at the last house on the short street, a boy his own size sat on the steps making a fishing pole.

"Hello," he said to Mike. "My name's Jake. What's yours? And where you from?"

"My name's Mike. I'm from the potato country down valley."

"Going to live here in Boulder?" asked Jake. He looked hopefully at Mike.

"Naw," said Mike, sticking his hands in his pockets. "We're going pioneering up in the redwoods."

The boy looked at him wide-eyed and then looked past him toward the evergreen hills. "Honest? You going up there? Boy, ain't you lucky!"

Mike stuck his chest out a little farther. "We'll do all right," he said.

"Want to go fishing?" Jake asked. "I'll cut a pole for you."

"Sure," said Mike. He went with Jake down to the river, and they cut another willow pole with Jake's knife. Then Jake pulled another piece of cord from his pocket, and Mike tied it to the pole. Jake searched in all his pockets and finally found a couple of bent pins.

They dug some worms for bait. Then Jake led the way down a faint path to a fallen log that stuck out into the river.

Mike had never been fishing before. The little creek that ran through the valley where their cabin had been didn't have any fish in it. But he wasn't going to let Jake know. He watched closely and then did exactly as Jake did. Soon he felt a jerk on his line. It was a fish! He held tight as the fish zipped back and forth. Finally he managed to pull it in. It was a foot-long trout.

"What a beauty!" Jake exclaimed. "You're lucky." In a few minutes he had also caught a fish.

Mike baited the pin again and in a few minutes had another trout, a bit smaller than the first. "I'll need several more to make enough fish for our family for dinner," he said.

"How many in your family?" Jake asked.

"Nine, counting Ma and Pa," said Mike. "I'm the middle one."

"You're lucky," said Jake. "I don't have any brothers or sisters."

"I guess that's even lonesomer than being the middle one," said Mike. He pulled in another big trout.

"The fish are biting good this morning," said Jake. "Sometimes the water wheel up at the mill makes so much racket it scares them away."

"This ought to be plenty," Mike said a while later. He counted the fish he had laid on the mossy bank. "Six big ones and one little fellow."

Jake sharpened two willow withes, and they strung the fish on them. Mike walked proudly up the path and past Jake's house to his camp.

Mary saw him coming. "Ma! Pa!" she shrieked. "Look what Mike's got!"

Ma straightened up from her packing, and Pa turned around.

"Why, Mike," said Ma, "did you catch those yourself?"

Mike grinned.

"Sure, and you're a real fisherman," said Pa. "Shall I help you clean them for dinner?"

Mike agreed to this. He didn't have the faintest idea how to fix them. With Pa's help, they soon had the fish ready for Ma's hot frying pan. Mike thought he had never had such a good dinner in his life. He hoped that when they found a place for their new cabin in the redwoods there would be a stream nearby with fish in it.

Chapter 5

A Midnight Visitor

In the afternoon Mike went with Jake to see the sawmill. They watched the big saws, as large as wagon wheels, slice the logs into lumber. After the saws had cut the logs into the straight red lumber, it fell into the flume. Water from the river came into the flume all the time and carried the boards away.

"It floats all the way to Felton," said Jake. "Then they dry it and take it to Santa Cruz. Then it goes on ships to San Francisco and other places."

They went around and looked at the mill pond where the logs were floating until they would be sawed. A heavy iron cable pulled the logs up a skid into the mill to the saws. Jake took Mike around the pond to the skidways, where the ox teams were hauling the logs to the pond.

"Aren't the logs huge?" said Mike.

"Big as a house," said Jake. "Look how those oxen strain to pull them."

"How do they cut such big trees?" Mike asked.

"The loggers won't let us come close to where they are working, but you can see some of what they do up there on that hillside." Jake pointed to where two men were sawing some distance away.

Mike strained his eyes to watch. He could see the two small platforms stuck onto the lower part of the tree, and the man standing on each one. They were using a long saw.

"They chop an undercut with the ax to make the tree fall the way they want," Jake explained. "And they make a saw cut on the side that it falls toward."

"The tree is so big I don't see how a thin saw cut would make it fall in any special direction," said Mike.

"Oh, they put in wedges," said Jake. "The wedges make it go in the right direction."

"The logs the oxen are pulling aren't as long as a whole tree," said Mike.

"They always buck them—"

"Buck?" Mike asked. "What's that?"

"Saw them into shorter lengths," explained Jake. "They peel off the bark, too, before they pull them to the millpond."

Mike looked at the hillsides beyond the sawmill. "The hills look dreadful with the redwoods cut off," he said. "Why do they burn the hillsides?"

"To clear the underbrush away so the logs can be hauled. But the hillsides do look terrible," Jake agreed. "But come with me," he added.

Mike followed him up a blackened, stump-covered hillside, wondering what Jake wanted to show him. Soon they came to a place where a young forest was growing up again.

"See," said Jake. "Cutting the trees doesn't always kill the roots. Look at this one."

They pushed through a ring of saplings. In the center was the stump of a tree that had been cut down.

"What a tree," said Mike. "First it was only one, now it's about ten. Will they really grow to be big redwoods?"

"Sure," said Jake. "You can hardly kill them. Why, I saw one great big tree that had fallen down some winter. A new tree was growing straight up from the roots that were sticking up in the air."

They tried skimming flat stones across the river for a while and then wandered back into Boulder.

"I hope you won't go too far up in the mountains," said Jake. "I wish you could stay right here. We could have loads of fun."

Mike nodded. "I'd like that. But Pa wants to go where the tan oaks are thickest. And besides, we came way up here because Pa likes to have lots of room to stretch—"

"He what?" asked Jake.

"He doesn't like to have neighbors," Mike explained.

Jake began to laugh. "What a funny idea. Doesn't your ma like to have neighbors, either? My ma likes to visit lots with the other women."

"Ma goes where Pa goes," said Mike. He really hadn't thought about whether Ma liked to be off in the wilds or not. She never complained about anything.

"I'd better be getting home," said Jake. "I have to milk the cow."

"Me, too," said Mike. "We'll probably leave real early in the morning, so I won't see you for a long while. Bye." He ran toward the tent. He wanted to get busy quick so he wouldn't think about how lonesome he would be way off in the redwoods. It was such fun having a friend, even for only a day.

They left Boulder the next morning as soon as it was light enough to see. The mist was still floating above the river. They left the San Lorenzo River and followed a wide creek.

There was no path or road now. Pa went first, with an ax over his shoulder to cut the brush where it was too thick to push through. He was leading one of the donkeys, loaded to its ears with their stuff.

Tom and Pat each led a donkey, too. Then came Ma, holding Liam by the hand, and Sean and Mary tagging

along as close as they could. Mike was next, leading Bossy, and Martha was last, leading Maury. Mike thought they looked like a bevy of quail playing follow the leader.

The walking was hard. They went uphill all the time. Sometimes they had to climb over fallen logs, or go around them. The brush tore at them, and some of it had nasty thorns. Mike got a long scratch down one cheek where a blackberry branch slapped him.

Before long Ma had to carry Liam. The going was too rough for him. Then she had to sit and rest often, for he was heavy.

"Couldn't he ride on Bossy?" asked Mike.

"Let's try it," said Ma. She set Liam on Bossy's broad back, and he held to Bossy's collar. Ma walked along beside him, so she could catch him if he fell.

The chickens didn't like riding donkey-back. They scolded and clucked. The donkey didn't like the scolding and kept tossing her head and flapping her ears.

Mike was glad when they stopped for the night. He was tired out from the climb. Pa cleared a space and started a fire, and Ma soon had a stew cooked. Mike laid out his bed after he had milked the cow.

While he was laying out his bed, he saw something crawling on a nearby redwood tree. He had never seen anything like it before. It was bright yellow and slimy-looking and about as long as his middle finger.

"Pa," he called. "What's this slimy thing?"

Pa came over to see. "That's a mountain slug, Mike. Sort of a snail without a shell."

Mary looked at it and shuddered. "Oooh! It's wiggly."

Then Mike had a terrible thought. "Pa, will it crawl into my bed tonight?"

Pa laughed. "Don't worry, Mike. That slug isn't interested in you at all. It only likes plants and trees."

Mike wasn't so sure. He snuggled down into the covers and went to sleep to dream about long yellow slugs creeping over him.

In the middle of the night, Mike woke up. He could hear little sniffing and nibbling noises. He wondered if it was a bear. But Pa had said there weren't any bears here. Mike was scared anyway.

Suddenly something went *crash!*

Mike sat up. "What is it?" He rubbed his eyes and tried to see in the thick mist and darkness.

Pa got up. "'Twas a deer, I think. He knocked over one of the bundles. Probably smelled the potatoes."

A deer! Right beside their beds. Mike shivered. That was better than a bear, but he wished he could take his bed inside the tent. But if he did that, everyone would laugh at him and say he was a scaredy-cat or a baby.

He decided he would be brave, for pioneers had to be brave. But he did pull the covers over his head. He didn't want any deer to mistake his hair for dry grass.

The next day they tramped and climbed. They pushed through brush and went around huge redwood trees. They saw more tan oaks than they had near Boulder. Mike did hope they would stop soon. He saw the most wonderful places to build the cabin. By suppertime when they stopped to camp, he was so tired that he knew he would never feel it even if a deer came and chewed his hair. All he wanted was to sleep and sleep and stop tramping through the forest.

Chapter 6

Timber!

Mike opened his eyes drowsily. Where was he? For a minute he stared up at the dim outlines of the tall redwood trees above him, their tops hidden in the fog. Then he remembered. He was two days' walk into the forest from Boulder.

He snuggled down in his warm covers under the shelter of a nutmeg tree and listened to the gentle drip of the spring mist in the forest around him.

He could smell the sweet perfume of the azalea trees by the creek. They smelled good enough to eat. He could barely make out the outlines of some tan oak trees a short distance away.

Mike hoped they would build their cabin here. He was tired of walking and climbing through the endless forest. Besides, last night when they had stopped to camp, he had seen a wide deep pool where the two creeks joined below their camp. Maybe there were fish in the streams. Anyway, the pool would make a wonderful swimming hole in the summer, whether there were fish or not.

He could hear Pa building the fire, and by turning his head he could see that Pat and Tom were already up. He climbed slowly out of his warm covers. He sat on the springy redwood duff and shivered as he pulled on his heavy new shoes and laced them up. He was glad he had them to wear these cold wet mornings in the forest. Back in the valley he hadn't bothered with shoes much.

Ma smiled and handed him the water pail. He made his way slowly through the drippy brush down to the creek. Balancing himself on two slippery rocks, he dipped the pail into the icy water. He would surely hate to fall into it.

Then he picked a cluster of the silvery azalea blossoms and took them to Ma. She tucked the flowers into her shiny black hair.

Her blue eyes sparkled when Pa said, "Sure, and you're still my wild Irish rose after these eighteen years. But it's been a long time since we sailed away from Ireland."

Mike grinned. He wished Pa would sing the song about the wild Irish Rose. Pa hadn't sung a bit for many, many days. Mike knew he was too anxious to get settled again to think about singing.

Mike sat as close to the blazing fire as he could while he ate his breakfast. The mist had stopped falling, but water still dripped from the lock of hair that hung over his forehead. He wished this wonderful redwood forest could be drier, but he knew it was the mist that made the redwoods grow so tall and thick.

Pa had gone off on a tramp through the trees and wet brush. Now he came back to the fire. He shook himself like a dog, and the fire sputtered from the drops of water that flew from his clothing.

"Can we build the cabin here, Pa?" Mike asked.

"Well," said Pa. "Did I see you looking at that swimming hole down in the creek last night?"

Mike laughed, and Pa smiled through his long whiskers.

"This would be a good place," said Ma. "There's water close, and the trees aren't too thick right here on this little ridge—"

"That's right," said Pa. "It's no joke to cut down a redwood."

"I'll bet we can build the whole cabin from one tree," said Pat.

"Sure, and I wouldn't be surprised," said Pa.

"There's no place here for the potatoes nor the garden," said Martha.

"No," Pa agreed. "The garden will have to go farther up the hill, away from the creeks. A garden needs more sunlight."

"It wouldn't have to be near the cabin, would it, Pa?" Mike was still thinking of that pool in the creek.

"We could fence the garden with brush," said Tom. "It wouldn't have to be near the cabin."

"I think everyone wants the cabin right here, then," said Pa. "Right?"

"Hurrah!" shouted Mike. He jumped up and down. Liam and Sean jumped up and down, too, and tried to say hurrah. Everyone laughed at them.

"I wish we could have a log cabin," said Mary. "Like the pictures in Ma's old book."

Pa laughed and slapped his knee. "A log cabin! Ha, ha! Why, Mary, if we built a cabin of these logs it would be so big that only a giant could live in it. Look at the size of those trees, honey-bug!"

Mary hid her face in her mother's dress when the older ones laughed at her.

"Never you mind," said Pa. "It's going to be a good snug house, and you and Martha will have a room of your own in it, too."

"What about all us boys?" asked Tom, trying to look jealous.

"You three oldest ones can sleep in the loft," said Pa, "and Sean and Liam will have a trundle bed."

"Oh, goody," said Mike. He was glad he wouldn't have to sleep in a trundle bed with Sean now.

Pa stood up. "This fire feels mighty good, but we've got real work to do. We've got to fell a redwood today, and that's one big job—"

"Oh, Pa, can I help?" asked Mike eagerly.

Pa shook his head. "I'm sorry, Mike, you're not big enough yet. Felling a redwood is dangerous business. You help Martha watch the little fellows to be sure they don't come near where we're working. But after the tree is down, you can help when we split it. All right?"

Mike bit his lip. He did want to see the tree fall, but he knew Pa was right. He looked up at the huge trees. He wouldn't want to be in the way when one came crashing down.

Pa and Tom and Pat shouldered their axes and long saw and marched off to find a good-splitting tree. After they had gone, Mike led each of the cows and donkeys to grassy places across the creek and tied them securely. He didn't want them wandering off to where the tree would fall.

He returned to the tent. Sean and Liam were still sitting by the fire. Mary was smoothing out the beds in the tent. Mike was glad to see the sun peeking through the misty fog.

"Come on, Sean and Liam," he said. "I know where there's lots of sand. Do you want to play?"

"Let me come, too," begged Mary.

"You are a real helper, Mike," said Ma. "Will you watch to see that they don't wander into the forest?"

"Sure," said Mike. "I'll stay right with them beside the pool in the creek. We can have lots of fun." He was glad he could help Ma, even if he wasn't big enough yet to do real pioneer work like Pat and Tom.

They trooped down to the pool where the two creeks joined. There was lots of sand along the bank, and the sun was shining on the pool. Mike showed the two little boys how to build castles, and they made boats out of twigs and floated them on the water. Mike watched the creek for fish, but they were all too tiny for him to bother with.

All morning they played. When Ma called them to dinner, Mike pulled a handful of horsetail weeds and took them up to the tent.

"Oh, Mike," said Ma. "Where did you find the scouring rushes? I've been wishing I had some to scrub the kettles."

"There are lots of them along the creek," said Mike. "I'll get you more when you want them."

After dinner they went back to the sand to play again. The sun was beginning to hide behind the tall trees on the hill when Mike heard Pat yelling.

"Tim-m-ber-r-r!" Pat roared. His voice echoed through the forest.

Sean and Liam covered their ears. Mike and Mary jumped up to listen better.

A minute later they heard it. Crash! There was a terrible rumble, and the ground shook.

Liam and Sean and Mary ran for the tent, shrieking and crying, "Ma! Ma!"

Mike grabbed the hands of the two boys. He didn't want them to go toward the tree. They were almost to the tent when Pat yelled again.

"Tim-m-ber-r-r!" Another crash and roar followed.

One of the donkeys jerked loose from the tree where Mike had tied her. Mike dashed after her, but she came straight for the tent. Mike tied her again and patted her head and talked quietly to her. He went to each of the other animals and talked to them. Soon they were eating grass again as if nothing had happened. The rooster was crowing and the hens were cackling, but Martha soothed them.

Soon Tom came marching toward the tent, looking big and strong, like a logger. "Pa says Mike can come now to see the tree," he said.

Mike started right out after Tom, and Ma grabbed up Liam, and then the others came, too. They all wanted to see the fallen redwood.

"Why did you chop two, Tom?" Mike asked, as he

stumbled after his big brother.

"We didn't," said Tom. "The second one happened to be in the way of the one we chopped. The one we chopped down loosened it, and it fell, too. Boy, my ears are still ringing!"

"I'll bet," said Mike. "It sounded like the loudest thunder I've ever heard."

"It was worse than the noise that train made in Santa Cruz," said Mary.

Mike gasped when he saw the size of the fallen tree. Tom helped him climb up the side of the huge log, and he stood up and walked along it. Why, if they could carve out the inside of the log, it would be a good house just like that.

Pa laughed and laughed when Mike said that.

"I think I'd rather have a board house," said Ma.

"I'm hungry," said Pat. "We haven't had a bite since breakfast."

"We'll leave the tree till tomorrow," said Pa. "Then we'll begin bucking and wedging and splitting the wood."

He mussed up Mike's hair. "And Mike, we're going to put you to work on this splitting job, too. How'll you like that?"

Mike grinned. There wasn't anything he would like more.

Chapter 7

Tree-Splitting

Mike was up the next morning as soon as the mist was light. He got the pail of water from the creek, and he milked Bossy. Pa and Ma and the older children were up working, too. There would be work for everyone building the new cabin and putting in the garden.

As soon as they had eaten breakfast, Mike went with his father and brothers to the redwood tree they had cut. They carried the heavy oak wedges and mallet. Mike knew what they were. But Pat had two other tools that he didn't recognize.

"What are those things?" he asked Pa.

"A bolting froe and a riving froe," said Pa. "They are used to split the timbers into boards and shakes. You see they are like heavy knife blades with a handle at one end at right angles to the blade." He took one of the froes from Pat and showed Mike how sharp it was. "And see the point of metal on the end of the blade opposite the handle.

"We push on that point with this club-shaped maul," said Pa. "By pushing with the maul and with the handle of the froe, we can split the timber easily."

"Easily?" said Pat. "It's still work."

Pa laughed. "I meant it was easier than splitting the timbers with an ax or a pocket knife."

When they reached the log, Pa and Pat began bucking it into the lengths they wanted. Mike helped Tom saw off the branches at the top of the log and then they pulled them away and piled them. They were heavy to pull. Mike's arms ached, but he didn't complain.

"How do you split the log, Pa?" Mike asked.

"First in half, with the big wedges," Pa said, going right on with his sawing. "Then into quarters. Then we take the sharp edge off the quarters and begin to split timbers with the mallet and gluts—the little wedges. Last, we split the timbers into boards with the froe and maul."

"Good thing redwood always splits straight," Pat puffed from the other end of the eight-foot saw.

"Lots easier to work with than any other wood," said Pa.

When Pa and Pat had cut off the first length of the log, Pa began to wedge the wood, while Pat and Tom went on with the bucking.

"How long will it take to build the cabin, Pa?" Mike asked.

"Several weeks," said Pa. He didn't even stop pounding the wedges when he answered.

Mike's ears were ringing from the loud ping noise the mallets made on the wedges. The noise echoed back and forth from the trees and the hills and sounded like a dozen hammers.

They worked from early morning until dark every day, pounding with mallets and splitting boards with the froe. By the end of the week, a pile of timbers and boards lay beside the unsplit part of the log.

"When will we begin to build the cabin, Pa?" Mike asked.

"Tomorrow you and Pat can level the ground," said Pa, stopping to look at the timbers. "I think you can do it in one day."

Mike danced a jig.

"Save your energy for working," said Pat, pounding another wedge into the log.

Pa continued. "Then the next day you and Tom and I can begin to put up the timbers for the house, and Pat can keep working here on the log."

"Got to split lots of boards for the siding," Pat said.

"And shakes for the roof," said Tom.

"And planks for the floor," said Pa. "It's too cold and wet here for a dirt floor."

Mike struggled to put another long board on the growing pile. It would be wonderful to have a cabin again, but he kind of liked to sleep outdoors on the ground now that he was used to it.

The next day Pat and Mike didn't go to the log at all. Pa marked out the space he wanted cleared and leveled. Pat chopped down two small trees. Mike dug around them so Pat could chop out as many roots as possible. They didn't want a redwood tree to grow up through the cabin.

Then Pat began to chop down the bushes, and Mike carried all the brush to a big pile. Later he would cut it into firewood and kindling and stack it to dry.

They dug out several big rocks. Mike rolled them off to one side. Pa might want them to put under the foundation timbers.

"This place doesn't look very level to me," said Pat. He squinted at the cleared space.

Mike tried to squint the way Pat did. He knew the space wasn't level without squinting, though, because he had rolled the rocks.

"We need a level," said Pat. "And we don't have any."

Mike scratched his head. "I know what we can do," he said suddenly.

"Tell me, quick," said Pat.

"Put water in a pan," said Mike. "When we get the ground level, the water will be up the same on all sides when the pan sits on the ground."

"A good idea, Mike!" Pat exclaimed. "Pa couldn't have figured out anything better himself. We can set the pan on a long board to make it work even better."

Mike beamed. Pat didn't praise him very often.

"Since you thought of it," said Pat with a wink, "I'll let you get the pan and the water."

Mike ran to the tent and got a bread pan from Ma. He poured it half full of water and carried it carefully to the cleared space. He set it down on the ground. The ground sloped so much that the water almost ran out one side.

"See," said Mike. "It works."

"Good," said Pat. He looked at all the ground they would have to dig. "You know, Mike," he said, "I didn't pack that plow on my back all the way from Boulder for nothing. We're going to level this the easy way."

Mike caught on right away. "I'll get one of the donkeys," he offered.

Mike went after a donkey while Pat got the plow and harness. Soon they were plowing the ground that was too high. Then they scraped the loosened dirt over to the low spots and packed it hard. Then Pat laid a board down, and they put the pan of water on it. The water showed that the ground was level.

"That's done," said Pat, "and look how much work we saved! Always remember to use your head, Mike. And use it before you begin to work. Saves all kinds of trouble."

Mike nodded soberly. He'd remember.

The next day they began to carry the timbers and boards from the log to the cleared space.

"Whew, this lumber is heavy!" Pat wiped the sweat off his face.

"It ought to be dried before we use it," said Pa. "But we can't wait that long. We need a cabin."

All morning they carried timbers. After dinner, Pat went back to the log to split boards. Mike helped Pa and Tom. They carefully marked out the corners of the cabin. Then they laid the foundation timbers.

The younger children stood nearby to watch. Mike felt big. He didn't have to stand and watch. He could help with the work.

By the end of another week, they had the rough framework of the cabin in place.

"It looks like a real house now," said Mike happily.

"We'll soon move in," said Mary. She was helping now, too.

Pa measured the boards, and Tom cut them. Mike carried them to where they would be used, and Pa nailed them. Mary handed him the square nails. Sean and Liam picked up all the little scraps of wood and used them to build tiny cabins and forts.

After supper, Pa and Pat and Tom split shakes for the roof by the light of the fire.

"Can't waste any time," said Pa. "We've got to finish this cabin and get to work cutting bark."

Mike looked up at the cabin, tall and pink in the firelight. He knew it wouldn't be long until they could move in.

Chapter 8

Mountain Garden

The cabin was almost finished. Pa said that he and Tom would work on it for a while by themselves.

"We must get the garden in," Pa said. "Vegetables don't have long to grow here in the mountains."

"Where'll we put the garden?" Pat asked.

"That's what we've got to find out," said Pa. "Today I want you and Ma and Mike to climb up the hill and see if you can find a place that will get plenty of sun and won't need too much clearing."

Pat shouldered his ax. "Come on, Mike," he said. "Let's be moving."

Ma tied a kerchief over her head while she told Martha what to fix for dinner. "I'm ready," she said.

Pat led the way, almost straight up the mountain. Mike puffed right along at his heels, and Ma was close behind.

"Go right to the top, Pat," Ma said. "We can look down and pick out a place."

"Right," said Pat.

They were able to climb fast without the little ones to slow them down. But sometimes Pat had to stop and chop the thorny bushes out of their way. That gave Ma a chance to rest.

The sun was shining almost straight down on them when they reached the top of the mountain.

"Aren't you glad the cabin is so far up the mountain, Ma?" Mike asked.

Ma looked at him to see what he meant.

"We don't have to climb so far to get to the top," Mike explained.

Ma and Pat laughed.

The air was clear and all the mist had disappeared. They could see over a hundred ridges and valleys.

Ma looked toward the west. "We can see the ocean!" she exclaimed. Mike thought she looked pleased.

"But we can't see Santa Cruz," said Mike, staring at the faraway bit of dark blue.

"No," said Pat. "That little piece of the ocean that we see must be about halfway between Santa Cruz and Pescadero."

Mike looked admiringly at Pat. How did Pat know all that? Why, he didn't even know there was a town called Pescadero.

Ma was turning around on the rock where she stood, trying to spot the best place for the garden. "It should be on a south slope," she said.

"Why?" Mike asked.

"The south slope gets the most sunshine," said Pat.

"Which way is south?" Mike asked. "That's west toward the ocean, so this way must be south." He pointed with his left hand while he faced towards the west.

"That's right," said Pat.

They walked around a bit on the mountaintop. The ground was rocky here. There were pine trees with funny, knobby cones to take to Liam and Sean. Pat said he'd take one to Mary.

They soon picked out a good garden spot that wouldn't need too much clearing. It was on a south slope, but the ground wasn't steep nor rocky.

"Couldn't ask for a better place," said Pat.

"I wish it could be closer to the cabin," said Ma. "It's a hard climb."

"I'll build a path," Pat assured her. "That's easier than clearing redwood forest off closer to the cabin."

"All right, then," said Ma. "This will do."

"When can we begin clearing the ground?" asked Mike.

"Today," said Pat. "We'll go back to the camp right now and get a bite to eat—"

"I hope so," Mike interrupted. "I'm empty. I was afraid you'd say we'd start working without anything to eat."

Pat laughed. "All you think about is your stomach, Mike."

"Now, Pat," said Ma softly. "I think you don't forget your meals very often, either."

Then it was Mike's turn to laugh.

"Anyway," said Pat, "after we eat, Mike and I will come back with a couple of axes and begin clearing. In a few days we can plant the seed, I reckon."

Pat marked the trail down the hill by cutting slashes in the bark of the trees every few yards. Going down the hill didn't take as long as going up.

That afternoon Pat and Mike took Mary back with them to the garden space. Pat chopped down the few trees that were in the way, and Mike chopped the bushes. He hadn't used an ax much for chopping down the shrubs, so he was slow and careful. Mary piled the brush at the edge of the garden land.

"We'll drive in stakes and make a fence with the brush," said Pat. "I hope that will keep away the deer. If it doesn't—" he stopped and grinned at Mike.

Mike wondered what Pat was thinking of.

"We'll let Mike sleep up here at night to scare away the deer," Pat finished.

Mike blushed under his freckles. He didn't like to be teased about the way he slept with his head under the covers so the deer wouldn't scare him.

When the sun began to set, Pat put his ax over his shoulder. "Come on, you two," he said. "We want to be down to the camp by dark."

Mary didn't need to be told twice. She dropped the load of brush she was pulling and darted after Pat. Mike gave one last swing at the bush he was chopping and then followed.

A few days later, Pat and Mike and Mary had finished clearing the garden space. They built a brush fence around the garden.

"That should keep out the deer until the vegetables are big," said Pat. "Then maybe we'll have time to build a better fence."

The next day Mike led one of the donkeys up to the garden, and Pat carried the plow.

"Won't it be nice to have fresh corn and cabbage and new potatoes again?" asked Mike. "I'm getting tired of venison and old potatoes."

"Mm-m," agreed Pat.

Back and forth across the slope they plowed the moist, black ground.

"Why don't you plow up and down, Pat?" Mike asked.

"Makes the ground wash away when the rains come," said Pat. "We have to be careful because there is so much rain here."

"We don't want this soil to wash away to the river and the ocean," said Mike. "We worked too hard getting it cleared."

Pat nodded and kept on plowing back and forth.

"Whee!" exclaimed Mike. "The garden really looks big now that it's plowed."

Ma came up to the garden with them when they had it raked and ready to plant. Mike carried the hoe and rake, Ma had the seeds, and Pat had the potatoes.

"Sure, and it takes lots of potatoes for our family," said Ma. "I hope there's enough eyes on those potatoes to plant what we need."

"I'm sure the sack weighs as much as a cow," said Pat when they got to the garden.

"You've done a good job, boys," said Ma, looking over the smooth black ground. "Pa'll be right proud of you."

Mike grinned and Pat looked pleased, too. Mike hoped Pa would come up soon and see the garden.

Mike sat down and sorted the little bags of seed. Ma had written little slips of paper with the names of the seeds and put them in each bag when she collected the seed the summer before. Mike read them off, "Turnips, radishes, cabbage, parsnips, peas, beans, greens, onions, carrots—Let's plant lots of carrots, Ma."

"You're my carrot-top for sure," said Ma.

"He looks more like a turnip or parsnip to me," said Pat, laughing.

"You're a towhead, too," declared Mike. "Anyway, there's nobody in our family with red hair—only black and white."

"That's right, Mike," said Ma. She was busily cutting potatoes into sections so Pat could plant the eyes.

"We'll put the corn at the top of the slope," said Pat.

Mike looked up with a question mark on his face.

Pat laughed. "I never saw such a question-bug," he said. "Mike has to know why I do everything."

"That's the way a boy learns," Ma said.

"Of course," said Pat. "See, Mike, the corn grows tall, and we don't want it to shade the other vegetables. The sun is always a little bit to the south, even when it is east or west. That makes the shadows go north."

"I see," said Mike. "So all the other vegetables will be on the south side of the corn—"

"Bright boy," said Pat. "You catch on fast."

After Pat had planted the long rows of corn, he planted the potato eyes, and the hills of squash, pumpkins, and melons and made the rows for the other vegetables. The sun was hot as they worked. Mike dropped the seeds into the rows as Pat made them, and Ma and Pat covered the seeds carefully.

"It's good growing weather," said Ma, fanning herself with her sunbonnet.

"If it keeps up, we'll have radishes to eat in a couple or three weeks," said Pat.

"Goody," said Mike. "I'd like some radishes with the stew and wild greens. I can hardly wait until the garden grows up."

Chapter 9
A Cabin at Last

Mike and Pat helped on the cabin again after the garden was planted. It really looked like a cabin now. The walls were finished with boards and bats, and the shakes were on the roof. The floor was laid, and the inside walls were built.

Tom had hunted along the creek until he found some good clay. Mike helped him make the adobe bricks for the chimney and the fireplace. Pa built a handsome fireplace, big enough for Ma to cook in.

"It would be nice to have a stove," said Ma.

"Someday you shall," said Pa. "One of those shiny black pot-bellied ones we saw in Santa Cruz. You shall have it before winter, too."

Ma's blue eyes sparkled. "The fireplace is nice, though," she said.

When the fireplace and chimney were finished, Pa stood back, looked at it, and scratched his head.

"What's the matter, Pa?" Mike asked. "It looks good to me."

"It looks good," Pa said. "But what's worrying me is the rain—"

"Will it all melt into a mud pie?" Mike asked. He thought that would be terrible. Who wanted a chimney to turn to mud just when a fire was needed most?

Pa rubbed his whiskers.

"Couldn't you build a house over the chimney, Pa?" asked Mike. He didn't like to see Pa worried.

Pat and Tom laughed. "What a little-boy idea," said Pat. "A house over a chimney!" He laughed and laughed.

"Now, Pat," said Pa, "don't be thinking it's so funny. We'll have to do something like that, or the whole thing will wash away. We'll have to make walls all around the fireplace and chimney and some sort of roof way up above it."

"Lucky for us that redwood doesn't burn well," said Pat. "Or our wood chimney would go up in smoke."

Pa built the walls and roof for the chimney, and soon Mike couldn't see the mud bricks at all from the outside of the cabin.

Mike helped Pat make the shutters for the windows and hang them.

"Someday we'll bring up some real glass windows from Santa Cruz," said Pat.

Then the cabin was finished. The whole family trooped inside and inspected the rooms. There was a big front room. Ma and Pa and Sean and Liam would sleep there at night. In the daytime it would be the living room. The little room which opened off the front room was a bedroom for Martha and Mary. The long kitchen was in the lean-to at the back of the house, and the rest of the lean-to was the big pantry. Mike ran up the ladder through the hole in the front room ceiling to the loft. The loft was the boys' bedroom. Mike thought it was wonderful up there.

But the cabin didn't have any furniture yet. So Pa and the rest of the family got busy and made it. They made a big table, for as Mike said, a big family of nine needed a huge table. They made chairs and benches and cupboards. They made big beds and middle-sized beds and a trundle bed for Sean and Liam that would fit under Ma and Pa's high bed. Pat even made a rocking chair for Ma.

"What a funny rocking chair," said Mike. "But it rocks, anyway."

"Sure, and it's very nice, Pat," said Ma, rocking slowly back and forth. "And I thank you very much, Son."

Pa built a porch across the front of the cabin, and another at the kitchen door. "That's to keep the mud out of the house," said Pa.

"This is a redwood cabin," said Mike. "Everything is redwood except the chimney and the fireplace, and they are covered with redwood."

"The redwood cabin in the redwoods," sang Mary. "Isn't it wonderful?"

Ma and Martha stuffed the mattress tickings with redwood needles and made the beds. The first night that Mike slept inside the cabin he felt as if he was being shut up in a box. It had been a long time since he had slept under a roof.

"I like the smell of the new redwood boards," he said to Pat and Tom in their big bed at the foot of his. "But I'll miss having the mist drip down on me."

"I won't miss it," said Tom. "I don't like to have the drip from the trees running down my neck."

"And just think, Mike," Pat said, "you won't have to worry about having a deer chew off your hair while you sleep!"

"Pooh!" said Mike. He turned over and went to sleep.

Chapter 10
Crawdad

Since the cabin was finished and the garden was growing, Pa and Pat and Tom made a trip to Boulder with the three donkeys to bring up the rest of their stuff. Ma was happy to have her linen tablecloths for special days, and her curtains and rag rugs. And there were the few books and the rest of the pots and pans. The cabin was really like home when everything was in place.

"And Mike," said Pat, "don't you ever say I don't like you." He handed Mike a special sack.

"My shells!" exclaimed Mike. "Oh, thank you, Pat."

Pat mussed up Mike's hair.

Mary's face began to pucker. "Where's my shells?" she whimpered.

"Well," said Pat, "I—"

Mary began to cry.

"Don't cry, lassie," said Pat. "We don't need any extra rain in the redwoods." He took a sack from another pocket and gave it to her.

Mary dried her tears on her apron. "Thank you, Pat. You're a good brother." She hugged him around his waist, which was as high as she could reach.

"Well, Ma," Pa said the morning after he got back from his trip to Boulder. "The place is all yours now. I've got to be getting to work."

"And what do you think you've been doing?" Ma asked with a twinkle in her eye.

"Playing at house-building for fifteen hours a day," said Pa. "But I've got to be cutting the tanbark right away, or it will be too late in the season. Pat will go with me at first."

"What about me?" Tom asked.

"I want you and Mike to build a cowshed and chicken coop," said Pa. "There's plenty of lumber piled where we split the log. After that's finished, you can clear a space for drying the tanbark. Then I'll take you with me, too."

Tom watched disappointedly as Pat selected two axes. "How do you cut the bark, Pa?" he asked.

"Why, they told me just how to do it at the tannery," Pa said. "First we gird the tree in two places to make a four-foot section of bark. This is the best piece, and we peel it off. Then we cut down the tree and strip off the rest of the bark in four-foot lengths." He put the ax over his shoulder and took the packet of lunch Ma handed to him.

"Then we stack the bark to dry," Pat went on. "Someday we'll make a sled from a couple of small trees to haul the bark on. In the fall we'll take it on the wagon to the tannery in Santa Cruz."

"You mean you'll take it from here to Boulder on a log sled?" Tom asked.

"Not all in one trip," said Pa. "We'll take some of it down green and stack it beside the wagon to dry."

"What do you do with the tree when the bark is off?" Mike asked.

Pa laughed. "That's for you to cut up into firewood."

"Oh." Mike hoped it wasn't as tough to work with as some of the live oak he had cut into firewood at their old cabin.

Mike and Tom watched Pa and Pat set off through the forest. Mike would have liked to go with them, but he thought it would be fun to build a cowshed, too. As soon as Pa and Pat were out of sight, he and Tom began carrying the boards from the place where the log had been. There was no log now, only the boards, bark, lots of splinters, and sawdust.

They built a long cowshed, and made stalls for the two cows and the three donkeys. They made a place to store hay, too, and a place for all the tools.

"Next year Pa will want to clear land to grow hay," said Tom. "This year he'll have to buy some in Boulder, and that will cost plenty."

"I'm glad there's grass along the creeks and among the trees," said Mike. "That will feed the cows and donkeys for the summer and most of the winter."

The night the cowshed was finished Maury's calf was born.

"We finished the shed just in time," said Mike. He patted the head of the wobbly brown and white calf.

The smaller children danced around watching the cow lick the calf and moo to her softly.

"Let's name her Redwood," said Mary. "We have a redwood house and redwood furniture, and we live in the redwoods. We need a redwood calf."

Tom and Mike leaned on the fence and laughed.

"Such a funny name to give a calf," said Mike.

"That's all right," said Martha. "Mary never has named a calf before. We've all had turns. Mike, you named the last calf that was born."

"But Pa sold her," said Mike.

"He will sell this one, too," said Martha. "She'll make a good milk cow, like her mother, and Pa'll get plenty of money for her."

"Please, let's name her Redwood," begged Mary.

"All right," said Ma. "I think that would be a nice name for the first calf born in the big forest. We'll call her Redwood."

"Red for short," said Mike.

The garden was growing fast, and to Mike's disgust, the weeds were also growing fast. He and Mary or Tom had to spend a day or two every week pulling out the weeds. He had to repair the fence, too, where the deer tried to push through to eat the corn.

"I never saw corn grow so fast," Tom said one night. "Why, it's already taller than Mike. I don't think it's ever going to stop."

"Maybe it thinks it's Jack's beanstalk," said Mike.

"Anyway, it's a good thing we didn't plant the beans with the corn," said Tom.

"Why?" Mary asked.

"The corn grows so fast it would pull the beans out of the ground," said Tom.

"Now, now, Tom," said Ma. "You mustn't be telling such tales to the little ones."

"Honest, Ma," said Tom. "It really would." But Mike could see the twinkle in his eye.

Mike kept busy chopping wood, too. Pa had made him the official wood gatherer. Mike was proud of the job, but he wished it didn't take so much time. He had to find dead trees to chop, and then get the wood back to the cabin and pile it neatly along the side wall of the cowshed.

Some afternoons Mike could play, but not often. He liked most to play in the deep pool where the two creeks joined. Now that the weather was warm, Ma let him splash in the water with Sean and Liam, and sometimes Mary.

Ma and Martha would bring their sewing or knitting and sit in the shade of the nutmeg tree beside the creek. Then Mike and the little ones would splash and dive in the icy water. Mike tried to learn to swim, but he wasn't sure how it was done. He could splash hard with his arms and legs and get across the pool, though.

Sean would shout, "I'll splash you, Mike!"

Then Mike would try to get across the deepest part of the water to the high bank. Bushes hung over the water on that side, and he could hide behind their branches. Then he would really splash the water across to Sean, and Sean couldn't splash him at all.

Some days when Sean and Liam played in the sand, Mike would stand still in the water, and the fish would swim close to him and nibble at his toes. He wished that there would be big fish so that he could go fishing as he had in Boulder. Pa said these fish were too little to bother with.

One day Sean and Liam were getting stones from the edge of the creek above the pool. They wanted to build a rock fort in the sand.

"Mike! Mike!" Sean shouted. "Come quick!"

Mike scrambled out of the water. He was sure Liam must be hurt.

"What's wrong?" he asked.

Liam was dancing around, pointing, and jabbering. Mike hurried to him.

"A crawdad!" he said. "A huge one!" He pushed it out onto the sand and they played with it for a while.

Later Mike tried to draw a picture of it in his old copybook. He had already drawn pictures of deer and squirrels and violets and trilliums and the bright-colored tiger lilies that were beginning to bloom along the streams. In the middle of the pages were the words he had learned to spell and write, and around the edges he had pictures.

Mike showed the crawdad picture to Pa at supper. Pa only needed to look once.

"Why, it's a crawdad," he said. "You drew a good picture, Mike."

Pat laughed at him. Pat was big and strong and rough. "Drawing is for girls, Mike," he said.

Mike closed his book and sat on it. He didn't want his drawings to be laughed at.

"Sh-h, Pat," Ma said. "Many great artists are men. Mike must go to school someday and learn to paint."

Mike felt better when Ma said that. But he decided he wouldn't show her and Pa his pictures when Pat was around. Pat didn't look as if he agreed with Ma at all.

It wasn't really the drawing that Mike liked the best. He liked to find out all about the creatures that lived in the redwoods. He had to watch them closely to draw them. But he was still afraid of the redwood forest. It was so big, and the trees were so tall and strong. He always felt like a beetle crawling on the ground when he walked among the giant trees. He wasn't afraid of the swift deer, or the squirrels, or the black-masked raccoons, or even the howling coyotes. Even the slimy yellow slugs didn't bother him anymore. It was the trees. Whenever he wandered into the forest, he wanted to tiptoe so that the trees wouldn't hear him. But he never mentioned it to anyone. He knew Pat would laugh at him, for Pat wasn't afraid of anything.

Chapter 11

Exploring Pie Creek

The summer flew by. The corn grew taller and taller. When the tassels finally showed at the top, Mike took a long pole and measured one.

"Thirteen feet high, Ma," he said. "Did you ever hear of such tall corn?"

"The soil is really rich," said Ma. "I heard people say in Santa Cruz that the corn would grow that high in the redwood country, but I never thought I'd see it."

"We never had it so high at our old cabin, did we?" Mike asked. He was already beginning to forget how things were in the little valley in the potato country.

"No," Ma said. "I think the tallest corn we ever grew was about ten feet. These tall stalks will make plenty of feed for the cows, too."

"We could get lost in this corn," Mike said. "It's trying to be as tall as the redwoods."

"It'll have to grow some yet, then," said Martha.

Ma had been keeping an eye on the berry bushes that grew along the creek. One day she told Mike and Mary to begin picking the blackberries so that she could make jam.

Of course, Mike knew the berries were ripe already. He had been trying a few once in a while when he was gathering firewood. He knew Ma didn't care. There were more berries than anyone knew what to do with. He and Mary picked the water pail full again and again. They picked so many that there were berries every day for breakfast and supper, and plenty for jam, besides.

One day Mike explored the creek below the garden that ran away from the cabin, toward the west. He found two different kinds of berries. He picked some and carried them to the cabin to show Ma.

"Huckleberries and gooseberries!" Ma exclaimed. "I didn't know there were any here in the forest. Can you get more?"

"Sure," said Mike. "And I promise to bring every gooseberry I pick."

Ma laughed softly and Martha giggled. The gooseberries were so puckery that even always-hungry Mike wouldn't want to eat them without sugar.

The next day Mike and Mary started off early. Mike carried two pails, and Mary had two big sacks.

"Don't get lost," cautioned Ma. "Remember to stay on the creek."

"We won't get lost," said Mike.

They walked up the path to the garden, then around it to the top of the hill where the pine trees grew. Then they started down a tiny creek that soon grew wider. Before long the creek widened even more, and the banks were a tangle of berry bushes. Close to the water, there were strawberry plants.

"We should call this Pie Creek," said Mary. "Because of all the pie berries that grow on it."

"You always want to name everything," said Mike, his mouth full of blackberries.

"You told Ma you'd bring back all the berries you picked," Mary teased. "And you're stuffing on them instead."

"That was the gooseberries," said Mike. "I'm not going to carry any blackberries back over that hill. We can pick them near the cabin."

They walked slowly down the creek, picking the best berries and exploring the nooks of the creek. Other creeks joined it on its way down the mountain. It became a small river, some places narrow and deep, and other places wide and shallow and shining over the sand.

In the spots where the redwoods shaded the water, they found tall ferns. Mike counted five different kinds. He closed his eyes and tried to think how they looked so that he could draw pictures of them when he got back to the cabin.

They were going steadily downhill all the time, following the creek. The sun was high overhead, and hot. The bees made a drowsy sound around the flowers, and a few birds twittered.

"Only one more sack to fill," Mike said. He put the sack that they had filled to overflowing on a high rock in the middle of the creek. He had left the buckets the same way after they were full. He knew they would be easier to find again that way.

"I'm glad we didn't bring any lunch," Mary said. "I'm so full of blackberries I couldn't eat another thing."

"I can still eat more blackberries," Mike declared. He spied a blackberry bush across the creek with the biggest fruit he had seen yet. He waded across and began eating. In a few minutes Mary was beside him, popping berries into her mouth as fast as he was into his.

"I thought you were full," Mike said.

"I got hungry watching you eat," said Mary.

"We'd better fill our other sack of gooseberries and huckleberries," Mike said. "The day is half gone."

They each swallowed another handful of blackberries and then started on. Soon they had the sack full.

"I'm tired," Mary said. "Can't we rest here on the sand a little bit?"

"All right." Mike put the sack down on the dry sand.

Mary stretched out on the warm sand and in a minute was fast asleep. Mike sat and dangled his feet in the cold water. Everything was quiet now that Mary wasn't chattering. He heard the gurgling song of the creek, and from somewhere there was a roaring sound, low and steady. It reminded him of the faraway sound of the ocean the night they stayed in Santa Cruz, but the sound didn't get louder and softer like the sound of the waves. He put his ear to the ground. Then he could hear it distinctly. Suddenly a thought struck him.

"Wake up, Mary," he said, shaking her.

She sat up and rubbed her eyes. "What's the matter?" she asked sleepily.

"I think I hear a waterfall," Mike said. "Let's find it."

Mary jumped up, ready to go. They left the berry bag on the sand and started quickly down the stream. Soon the roar was louder, and Mike was sure it was a waterfall. Suddenly they came to it. The water jumped over three ledges and splashed into a pool at the bottom.

They made their way carefully to the foot of the falls and looked up.

"It's like sunshine falling over the rocks," Mary said in delight.

"The yellow rocks behind the water make it look like gold," said Mike. But he was disappointed. He was sure from the roar that the falls would be bigger. "I think there's another waterfall," he said.

They went farther downstream. Another creek joined the one they were on. And then Mike almost fell head first off the cliff when they came abruptly to the second falls. Holding onto bushes, they leaned over and looked. This was more beautiful than the first. The fine mist and spray blew into their faces.

"This one is like Ma's white lace curtains," said Mary.

Mike led the way carefully around the steep cliff and down to the base of the falls. They stood on a fallen redwood and watched the rainbows in the water where the sun shone on it.

"This still isn't enough for the roar," said Mike. "There must be another waterfall yet. Come, let's go a bit farther."

Mary followed obediently. The way wasn't so steep now, and Mike didn't see any signs of a cliff ahead that would mean another waterfall. But he still felt that the roar came from ahead of them.

Then, as they rounded a curve in the wide stream, and the thick redwoods shut off the sound of the falls behind them, Mike was sure. The roar was like the noise of thunder.

"Mike, it scares me. Let's stop here," Mary pleaded. She covered her ears with her hands.

"Come on," said Mike. He was entranced with the sound of the water. He had to see the falls. Mary followed timidly.

Then they saw it. Mike gasped. He had never expected to see a waterfall like this. They hurried down the slope and around to a spot where they could look straight at the falls.

They just stood and stared. Even Mary couldn't talk for once. Mike gazed first at the wide stream that rushed toward the overhanging cliff and roared off in a wide white torrent down, down to the big blue-green pool. A bright rainbow shimmered in the foamy spray.

Finally Mike turned away. This was even more than he had hoped for. Mary shouted above the sound of the water, "I'm glad we came."

Mike nodded.

Then a glance at the sun made his heart sink. "Mary, it's the middle of the afternoon! We'll really have to hurry now."

He led the way rapidly upstream. He could hear Mary puffing as she tried to keep up with him. He knew he mustn't wear her out; she wasn't used to such climbing.

Finally they came to the sandy place where they had left their last sack of berries. Mike picked it up, and they went

on. But Mary had to stop and rest often. Mike stood and waited impatiently each time. The sun was getting lower and lower in the west. The shadow of the mountain was over most of the creek. They picked up the second sack of berries.

"Mike, will we get back before dark?" Mary asked. She looked frightened.

"I hope so," said Mike. But he was sure they wouldn't. Mary was so tired. If he were alone, he could go much faster. He shouldn't have taken her down to the waterfalls.

Each place where the streams forked Mike checked to be sure he was going the right way. But that took extra time. There were so many places that he couldn't remember all of them. Then he would have to look for their footprints in the sand or along the damp bank. Mary sat down and rested each time while Mike made sure.

Mike was tired himself, but he didn't tell Mary so. She was almost ready to cry, and he didn't want to make her feel worse. He kept pushing on, always uphill as they followed the creeks. He picked up the first of the two buckets. Walking was a struggle then, with a bucket in one hand and the two heavy sacks in the other.

They could see the pink-orange glow of the setting sun on the tops of the mountains. Mike knew it was a long way to the cabin yet. If only they could get to the garden by dark, they could find their way down the path from there all right.

Tears were trickling down Mary's cheeks when Mike turned to see if she was coming. "Mike," she sobbed, "we'll get lost, and a bear will eat us up." She cried louder.

Mike put his bucket and sacks down and hugged her. "Don't cry, Mary," he begged. "Pa says there aren't any more bears here. We won't get lost. Stop crying now, so's we can go on."

Mary wiped her face on her dusty skirt. She looked so funny Mike had to laugh. Finally she smiled at him. Mike picked up the berries again, and they started on. The berries were getting heavier and heavier. Mike knew that when they came to the last bucket, Mary would have to carry one of the sacks. He wouldn't be able to carry any more.

The forest was dusky now. It was hard to be sure they were following the right creek all the time. Mike was relieved when they came to the other bucket. He was sure then that they were on the way to the cabin.

They trudged up the creek, stumbling over rocks in the twilight. Mike held the buckets carefully so the berries wouldn't spill. He watched hopefully for pine trees that would show they were near the mountaintop, but all he could see were the silhouettes of the redwoods against the deep-blue sky. A few stars twinkled, but they seemed a long way off.

Mary sat down on a rock. "I can't go another step, Mike," she cried. "I'm too tired to walk." She buried her face in her skirt and sobbed.

Mike didn't know what to do. He couldn't leave her there, and he couldn't carry her. He wished he could shout loud enough for Pa to hear.

Mike heard a sniffing noise, a faint sound. Mary heard it through her crying. She grabbed Mike's hand.

"What is it, Mike?" she whispered.

Mike was trembling, but he wouldn't let Mary know. "Only a deer," he said.

Mary stood up. She was ready to go on. She hadn't slept under the stars while they were camping, and she didn't want to start doing it now. Mike was glad the deer had scared her. At least, he hoped it was only a deer.

At last they were on the mountain top. It was much too dark to see, but Mike felt his way down to the brush fence around the garden. Then he was able to find the path. Even Mary was able to hurry as they trotted down the path.

Soon they saw a light through the trees. Ma had lit the kerosene lamp and put it outside on a stump. The candles were burning in all the windows. They ran toward the light and halfway down the path came right into their father's arms.

"Oh, Pa—" and Mary began to cry. Pa lifted her up to his shoulder with one arm, and took one bucket and the two sacks in his other arm.

"Will you make it, Mike?" he asked.

"Sure, Pa, I'm all right." Mike ached in every bone, but he was too happy to be back home to care about that.

Ma greeted them quietly. "I've been worrying about you, Mike." She ladled out two big dishes of stew for them. "But what beautiful gooseberries you've brought. Tomorrow I'll make pies."

Mike ate the stew like a donkey on a fresh pasture. He didn't know he was so starved. Poor Mary ate a few bites and slumped over sound asleep.

"Poor child," said Ma. "She's worn out. Where did you go, Mike?"

Pa carried Mary into the little bedroom, and Martha dressed her for bed. She didn't even stir as Martha tucked her in.

"We went down a creek on the other side of the mountain," Mike said between bites. "There were lots and lots of berries." He took another big mouthful. "Then when we had all the berries, we heard a waterfall. Oh, Pa, I wish you could see it!"

Pat and Tom came in. "Howdy, lost, strayed, or stolen one!" Pat teased. "We're glad to see you back now that we've finished your milking for you!"

Mike grinned.

"Sh-h," said Ma. "You'll wake Sean and Liam."

"Not Mary, though," said Martha. "You couldn't shake her awake!"

"There were three waterfalls, Pa," said Mike. His eyes were shining as he told about them.

Pa nodded. "You're quite an explorer, Mike. But next time you want to explore, take Pat or Tom or me with you, and leave your little sister home."

Chapter 12

The Little Irish Rose

Mike woke up with a start. He lay very quietly wondering what had awakened him. He could see through the window in the loft that the sky was still dark. Pat and Tom were both sleeping.

Then he heard the quiet talking of Martha and Pa downstairs, and a murmur from Ma. Ma hadn't been feeling well in the evening. Pa had moved the trundle bed into the girls' room so that the little fellows wouldn't disturb her. Martha had served supper, and Ma hadn't even got out of bed to eat.

Mike slipped out of bed and tiptoed to the opening in the loft floor. He looked down to the front room below. He couldn't see anyone, but he knew they were moving about from the flickering shadows he could see on the floor.

He heard an uncertain little cry, then a stronger wail. The new baby! Ma sighed, and Mike heard Pa kiss her. He could hear Martha saying a little prayer, too. He wanted to go down, but he knew Pa wouldn't like it.

He tiptoed back to bed and tried to sleep. He could hardly wait until morning to find out if the new baby was a boy or girl. But it didn't really matter. He wouldn't be the middle one anymore. Maybe Pa would call him one of the big boys, as he did Tom and Pat. He dropped off to sleep for a little while. When he woke again, the little piece of sky in the loft window was gray. He could hear soft footsteps below. He crept out of bed and dressed without waking Pat or Tom. Probably Pat wouldn't be interested, anyway. There had been six new babies since he was born, and this made seven.

Mike went down the ladder without making a sound. The front room was dark, but he could tell that Ma was asleep. He went into the kitchen. A candle was burning on the table, and Mike could smell the pot of coffee Pa had. Pa didn't have coffee often, because they hadn't brought much from Santa Cruz. But Pa must have thought this was a special occasion. Martha had her head down on her arms on the table. Mike thought she was asleep. The redwood cradle Pa had carved was standing by the table. All Mike could see in it was the patchwork quilt Martha had made. Then Mike stepped on the floorboard that always squeaked.

Pa turned. He smiled wearily at Mike and beckoned him to come on.

Mike tiptoed over to the table. "Is it a boy or girl?" he whispered.

"A girl," said Pa, grinning.

Martha raised her head and looked at Mike. She turned the little quilt back so that Mike could see the baby's face. It was even redder than the redwood cradle. Mike didn't remember that Liam and Sean had been so red when they were born, and he couldn't remember about Mary at all. Maybe little girls were supposed to be redder than baby boys.

Martha smiled at the puzzled look on his face. "Babies are supposed to be red," she said.

Mike took the milk pails and stepped out into the mist. He would surprise the family this morning and milk both cows before Tom could get out to do his share. Mike was going to prove that he was one of the big ones now.

Everyone was awake when he returned to the house a while later with the two heavy pails of warm milk. Even the baby had her cloudy blue eyes wide open. Pa had set the cradle beside Ma's bed.

"What will her name be?" Mike asked, as he joined the others around the cradle.

"Let's name her—" Mary began.

"Not Redwood," Pat interrupted. "You named the calf that!"

The others laughed.

"I wasn't going to say that," Mary pouted.

"And besides," Martha said, "Ma and Pa will name her."

"She is to be named Rosie," said Pa. "After my wild Irish rose." He smiled fondly at Ma.

Mike thought Ma looked pretty, propped up on the pillow with her hair in two long, shiny black braids.

Mary clapped her hands. "Rosie is a wonderful name."

"She's a real wilderness baby," said Mike.

Ma smiled. "You were a wilderness baby, too, Mike. Not a redwoods baby, though. But then years ago, almost ten, when you were born, the potato country was all wild, with clumps of redwoods and oaks and cottonwoods instead of potato fields."

"And there wasn't any railroad to Santa Cruz," said Tom.

"Santa Cruz wasn't even a town," said Pat. "I remember it. It was only a muddy little village, and half the people in it spoke Spanish."

"Almost half, anyway," said Martha. "Why, the Civil War was going on when Mike was born."

"And there wasn't any railroad to join California with the East," said Pat. "Everyone had to come by boat around the Horn, as we did."

Mike's eyes opened wide. He had almost forgotten the stories Pat used to tell him about the long, long boat trip from the East. Pat hadn't been very old when he made the voyage, and Martha and Tom were hardly more than babies. And now that he tried to remember, he could faintly recall the stories Ma used to tell of the voyage she and Pa had made from Ireland to the United States even before Pat was born. It seemed to Mike that Pa must have always been moving his family to keep in the wilderness. As fast as he settled in one place, other families would settle around him. Then he would pack up and move on. Ma said that their years in the potato country were the longest they had lived in any one place.

Sean and Liam had been watching the baby without saying a word. Their big blue eyes followed every aimless move the tiny hands made.

Then Rosie began to cry. Her hands stiffened, her face wrinkled, her mouth opened wide. And she was redder than ever.

Sean covered his ears with his hands. There was a pained expression on his face. "Why does she cry so *loud*?" he asked.

Pat laughed. "You did better than that, my boy!"

Sean stared at him. "Me? Cry that loud?"

"Indeed you did," Pat assured him.

"I wanted a brother," said Liam. "Not another sister to boss me like Mary does."

"You have lots of brothers," said Mary. "Martha and I needed another girl in the family."

Martha was holding the baby over her shoulder, patting her gently. She had stopped crying, and one hand had caught on Martha's thick braid.

"She's hungry," said Martha.

"So'm I," said Sean.

"Me, too," said Liam.

"All of you shoo into the kitchen," said Pa. "We'll have our breakfast, and Ma can give Rosie her breakfast, too."

Chapter 13

Mike's Caterpillar

Mike walked through the front room into the kitchen, after taking a peek at Rosie in her cradle. Ma was busy making stew. Sean and Liam were standing up on benches watching, and Mary was snitching the bits of venison and vegetables that spilled outside the kettle.

"Ma," Mike began, "do you have a jar or something that I could keep this caterpillar in?" He opened his hand a crack and showed her the wiggling gray and blue caterpillar.

Ma dropped her paring knife.

"Oh, dear," said Martha. "What next?"

Ma frowned at her. "It's a beautiful caterpillar," she said. "Keep it away from the stew, though."

She searched in the pantry and finally brought out a glass jar with a cracked top.

"Thanks, Ma," said Mike. "Give it to me, quick. He's trying to crawl up my sleeve." He gently lowered the caterpillar into the jar.

"Isn't it nice?" asked Sean.

"It's nice," echoed Liam. He put his chubby hand into the jar to pet the fuzzy back.

"Don't!" said Mike. "You'll squash it!"

"I won't," Liam said indignantly. "I like it."

"I'm going to keep it on the table in the front room," said Mike. "I want to watch it grow."

"Suppose it gets out and crawls into the baby's cradle?" Ma asked.

"Please keep it in my room," begged Mary. "I'll let you watch it whenever you want to."

Mike looked at Martha to see what she thought. After all, the room belonged to her as much as to Mary.

"All right," said Martha. "But it had better not get into our bed."

"I don't want Rosie to eat my caterpillar," said Mike. "So I think I'll put it in Mary's room."

He marched into Mary's room, followed by Mary, Sean, and Liam. He put the jar on the tiny table in the room, and then they all stood around the table. The caterpillar crawled around and around.

"What are you going to name him?" asked Mary.

"That's all you ever think of," said Mike. "You named the calf and the creek, and you wanted to name the baby."

"Name him Liam," said Liam.

"Aw, no," said Mike. "He doesn't look like you. He's fuzzy and blue and gray—"

"Liam is fuzzy-haired and blue-eyed," said Mary.

"But he isn't gray," said Mike. "And he runs instead of wriggling."

"I know!" Mary clapped her hands and danced a jig. "Call him Wriggly."

"Oh, all right," said Mike. "You would be the one to name him. Ma, I'm going to name my caterpillar Wriggly."

Ma came to the door of the room. "That's a nice name. Are you really going to keep him?"

"Of course," said Mike. "What does he eat?"

Ma sighed. "The garden mostly. Where did you find him?"

"On the tiger lilies by the creek." Mike dashed out the front door and down to the creek. He grabbed some lily leaves and ran back to the caterpillar.

Mike dropped a few of the leaves on top of the caterpillar. He wriggled out from under them and began eating fast.

"His mouth wriggles," said Mike. He put his face close to the jar and squinted at the caterpillar.

"Don't be so snoopy," said Mary. "Don't you think he likes to eat in peace?"

"The whole family watches me eat," said Mike. "Ma watches to see that I chew with my mouth closed, and Pa to see if I cut up my food, and Martha to see if my hands are clean, and Pat to see that I don't eat too much and not leave any for him, and Tom to see that I eat with the fork instead of the spoon, and—" He stopped, out of breath.

"And all the little ones watch so they can copy you," finished Martha, laughing.

"You should put sand in the jar with the caterpillar," said Ma.

"I'll get sand," said Liam. Before Mike could stop him, he had run to the creek and come back with both fists full of sand. He dumped it right on top of the caterpillar.

"Liam, you naughty boy!" exclaimed Mike. "You'll smother him." He dumped the caterpillar and sand out onto the table. Wriggly wriggled out of the sand. Mike put the sand into the jar, and then put the caterpillar and the leaves in.

Every spare minute the next few days Mike watched the caterpillar. Pat had told him that caterpillars shed their skins, and he wanted to see for himself how they did it. The caterpillar had eaten so much that he looked as if he would pop. Suddenly his furry coat did pop!

"Ma!" shouted Mike. "Mary! Sean! Liam!"

They all ran in quickly.

"He's shedding his skin," said Mike.

"Poor caterpillar," said Liam. "He'll be dead."

"He's supposed to shed his skin," said Mike. "Isn't he, Ma?"

"Yes," said Ma. "And sometimes I wish all of you could shed your clothes and grow new ones, too." She looked at Mike's pants that hardly reached to his ankles now.

Soon the caterpillar had shed his blue and gray coat and had a new brown and black one.

"He is prettier than he was before," Mary said when the caterpillar was dry and fuzzy again.

One day Mike came in to bring some fresh leaves to the caterpillar. It was gone.

"Ma!" shouted Mike. "Wriggly's gone!"

"Oh, dear," said Ma. "I suppose it is in the baby's cradle." She carefully turned back each cover, but the caterpillar wasn't there.

Mike stood in the middle of Mary's room. He wondered if Liam had taken the caterpillar.

"Why don't you look for it?" asked Ma.

Mike leaned over and looked under Mary and Martha's bed. The caterpillar wasn't there. The others put their heads down on the floor, too. They couldn't see the caterpillar either. Ma didn't put her head down on the floor. She said she didn't feel like leaning over that far. She began looking on Mary and Martha's bed. Right in the middle, on a brown and white nine-patch, was Wriggly, curled up sound asleep.

Mike put the caterpillar back into the jar and gave him the leaves.

"Now, Mike," Ma said. "If you don't keep that jar covered, you'll have to take Wriggly away."

"I'll be more careful, Ma," Mike promised. He didn't want to lose his precious caterpillar. It was almost the best treasure he had, next to his shells, and his rocks and cones and burls and polished bits of redwood, his tan oak acorns and pictures, and the little king snake in the redwood cage under his bed.

The next day, while Mike watched, the caterpillar began spinning a cocoon all around himself, and he settled down for a long sleep. Mike put the jar in the loft under his bed. Every day he looked at Wriggly. A week later the cocoon was beginning to wriggle again.

"Ma! Mary! Sean! Liam!" shouted Mike, dashing down the ladder. "The cocoon is waking up!"

"And so is the baby," said Ma, as Rosie began to cry. "Can't you be quieter in the cabin, Mike?"

"I'll try," said Mike. He really was sorry he had awakened the baby. He put the jar on the kitchen table, and even Martha sat down to watch the caterpillar.

The cocoon wriggled and split. At last Wriggly began to push out the end of the cocoon. He crept out and clung to the leaf.

"He isn't a caterpillar anymore," said Mike.

"He's a butterfly!" Liam clapped his hands gleefully.

"He has white wings with black spots," said Mary. "We should call him Spotty, now."

Mike didn't pay any attention. He was thinking about catching some more caterpillars to see if he could raise some other butterflies before the rainy weather began.

Chapter 14

The Stranger

Mike had been very busy for several days. The vegetables in the garden were ready to harvest, and it turned out that he was chief harvester. Pa, Pat, and Tom were away every day gathering tanbark. Sometimes they were away two or three days at a time. Often they took the donkey-loads or sled-loads of the bark directly to Boulder and stacked it on the wagon, but sometimes they brought it to the cabin to dry. Mike wished he could go along on the trips to Boulder so that he could see Jake, but Pa said no. Pa said that Ma needed Mike to help her, especially now that she had the new baby to look after.

Mike had dug the baskets and baskets of fat potatoes and stored them. He had pulled and dried the onions and put the corn in the corn crib until they could have it ground into meal. He had stacked the round orange pumpkins in the pantry, along with the big green hubbard squash. He had put the dried beans and peas into neatly tied sacks.

He was glad now to have a little vacation before he had to harvest the winter supply of carrots, turnips, cabbages, and other vegetables. This afternoon he meant to search for more cocoons to keep in a dark box until spring.

He went slowly down the stream, looking on the backs of the lily leaves and on the bushes for the cocoons. He had found three different kinds already, besides two kinds he had found in the garden when he was harvesting the vegetables.

He came to a place where the stream widened and there was a dry sandbar. The warm sand looked so inviting that Mike stretched out in the sunshine and looked up at the blue sky above. All around him the redwoods towered. They seemed more friendly now that he knew them better. From where he lay, they looked tall enough to catch the tiny white clouds that floated across the sky.

The bees and other insects made a drowsy sound, and the creek murmured sleepily. Mike's eyes began to droop shut, and soon he was sound asleep.

Suddenly he awoke. He sat up and glanced around trying to see what had awakened him. Then he heard a soft pad-pad noise. His eyes darted this way and that, trying to see what had made the noise. He knew it couldn't be Pa and the boys coming back to the cabin yet, for it was only the middle of the afternoon.

The sound seemed to be coming closer. He was sure it couldn't be a deer, nor either of the cows, and Pa had all three donkeys. He stepped quietly into the shadows of the redwoods and waited. He didn't feel afraid as he had when they first came to the redwood country. He was only curious.

A tall man with a pack on his back came into sight across the stream. Mike watched him without speaking. The man came down to the stream bed and looked around. If he noticed Mike's footprints on the sand, he did not

show it. Mike watched him catch a large butterfly in a net. The man examined the butterfly, and then let it go. He stooped and took a drink from the creek and then stood up and looked around.

Mike wondered what he should do. He wished Pat or Tom were with him. They always knew what to do and say, but Mike was shy. He had seen too few people in his life to be at ease with a stranger.

But finally his curiosity got the best of his shyness. He wanted to know why this stranger was here catching butterflies. He stepped out of the shadows.

"Hello," he said.

The stranger turned toward him quickly. "Howdy, young fellow. Glad to see you." He smiled at Mike. "You're one of the O'Grady boys?"

Mike nodded solemnly. "I'm Mike O'Grady, sir."

"I'm Hiram Downs," said the stranger. "I'm a naturalist. They told me in Boulder that I'd find your cabin up here."

"I'll take you to it," said Mike. He wondered what a naturalist was, but he was afraid it wasn't polite to ask. He picked up his little box of cocoons and started up the creek toward the cabin. The stranger followed.

Soon they came to the deep pool where the two creeks joined. The younger O'Gradys were wading and laughing as they splashed the cold water around.

"Hello, children," Mr. Downs said.

Mary clapped her hand over her mouth and dashed up the path toward the cabin. Sean and Liam followed her like two frightened fawns.

"Not used to black-bearded strangers, are they?" the man asked Mike. He laughed as chubby Liam tried to scramble up the steep path.

Mike stepped lightly across the creek on the rocks. The man followed him slowly, balancing carefully in his heavy boots. When they reached the top of the steep bank, they could see Ma and Martha standing on the porch, with Mary, Sean, and Liam all trying to hide behind Ma's skirts.

Mr. Downs bowed slightly toward Ma and took off his hat. He introduced himself again.

"Mike," Ma said. "Bring my rocking chair out here on the porch so Mr. Downs can rest."

While Mike got the chair, Martha poured a glass of cool buttermilk from the churning of that morning and took it out to the visitor. He drank it gratefully.

"It's hot weather we've been having, for the redwood country," Ma said.

Mr. Downs agreed. "But it's cool here compared to San Jose and the valleys beyond," he said.

Ma soon excused herself to feed the baby and fix supper.

"Don't go to any trouble for me," Mr. Downs said. "I'm used to roughing it."

Ma didn't say anything, but Mike knew they would have an extra-special supper. They didn't have company often. In fact, they hadn't had any company since they moved to the redwoods.

He settled himself on the steps to watch the stranger. Mr. Downs had picked up a stick of redwood that was lying on the porch and was carving it with his shiny pocket knife. Mike wondered what he would make. Sean and Liam kept creeping closer to watch.

Then Mike knew what it was. It was a boat, only as long as Mike's hand. Mr. Downs smoothed it with his knife and then handed it to Sean. Sean grinned shyly and hugged the boat.

"What do you say to the man, Sean?" Mary asked.

"Thank you," Sean muttered with a wider grin. He dashed down the path to try the boat in the pool.

Liam's face puckered, and the tears rolled down his cheeks. "I want a boat, too," he wailed.

"Hear, hear," Mr. Downs said. "I'll make you one if you'll find me a dry stick."

Liam ran around the house to the woodpile and returned with a heavy chunk of redwood.

Mr. Downs laughed. "You want a battleship, don't you, sonny?" He split the wood into smaller pieces with his knife, and soon had carved another boat almost like Sean's.

Liam was delighted. "Thank you," he shouted, not at all shyly. He ran down the path to join Sean at the pool.

The man considered the redwood sticks he had split and then chose a thick one. Mike wondered what he would make this time. Slowly the stick began to take shape.

"A doll!" Mike exclaimed.

Mary peeked around the back of the chair to watch. Soon the man handed her the doll.

"Will you name it Redwood?" Mike teased her.

"No," Mary said. "I'll name it Rosie, like the baby." She wrapped her kerchief around it like a blanket and sat on the steps rocking it and humming a lullaby.

"Mr. Downs," Mike began, then stopped.

"What did you want to know?" the man asked.

"What is a naturalist?" Mike just couldn't wait until Pa came to find out.

"A person who studies birds and flowers and trees and animals," Mr. Downs said. "I've been exploring the redwood country all summer to see the different kinds of trees and other things that grow here."

"Is that why you caught the butterfly?" Mike asked.

"Why, yes. Did you see me?"

Mike nodded. "I was watching you from the shadow of the trees."

Mr. Downs reached into his pack that he had set beside the chair. He pulled out a thick notebook and opened it. "You see, going by myself through the forest, I can't carry specimens of all the birds, insects, and plants. So I make drawings of them." He opened the notebook and showed Mike a colored drawing of a butterfly. "I already had a picture of that butterfly, so after I examined it, I let it go."

Mary looked at the pictures, too. "Mike draws pictures like that," she told Mr. Downs.

Mike could feel his face getting warm under his freckles when Mr. Downs looked at him. He didn't like Mary to tell his secrets.

"He draws wonderful pictures of snakes and birds and animals and butterflies," Mary rattled on. "And he has cocoons and caterpillars and nests and shells and rocks—" she stopped, out of breath.

Mike wanted to crawl under the porch and hide. Suppose this man laughed at him like Pat always did? But Mr. Downs was looking at him kindly, not laughing at all.

"Could I see your drawings?" he asked.

Mike went into the house and ran up the ladder. He came down a minute later clutching his precious copybook. He did hope Mr. Downs wouldn't make fun of his drawings.

Mr. Downs looked through the book slowly. He named each animal and bird and most of the butterflies and plants as he looked at them.

"Would you write down the names for me?" Mike asked, forgetting about being laughed at. All he could think of now was this wonderful chance to learn more about the wild creatures.

Mr. Downs printed the names of the animals and plants in each of Mike's drawings. "You've done well, son," he said. "You have drawings of some birds and insects that I haven't seen yet. Mind if I copy them?"

Mike was thrilled to think this man wanted to copy his pictures. He stood beside the rocking chair to watch him sketch the pictures quickly.

"Do you remember the colors?" Mr. Downs asked, taking a package of colored pencils from his pack.

"Oh, yes," said Mike.

Mr. Downs handed him the pencils, and Mike colored his own pictures. Then Mr. Downs copied the colors on his drawings.

"I'd like to be a naturalist someday," Mike said. "Could I be?"

"Indeed you could," said Mr. Downs. "You're off to a good start. You keep watching for everything in the forest, and learn all you can. Then, when you're old enough, you can go to college and learn more about science. Someday this country will need many naturalists for teachers and to take care of the forests. Maybe you'll be able to help."

"I hope I can," said Mike. His eyes were shining. He hadn't known before that grown folks studied about the forest creatures.

The smell of the supper was drifting out the door to them, and Mike suddenly remembered that he hadn't had a thing to eat since dinner. He hoped that Pa and Pat and Tom would come soon, or he'd have to grab a bite before supper. He hoped Ma would make shortcake, to eat with blackberries and cream. Um-m. The thought made him hungrier than ever.

Finally they heard the braying of the donkeys, and Pa and the boys trooped down the garden path with the loads of bark. Mr. Downs went to meet them.

Mike hung back. He could tell that Pa liked Mr. Downs at once. Maybe Pa would ask him to stay several days. Mike hoped so.

Mike and Tom fed the donkeys and milked the cows. Mike was getting hungrier by the minute. When Tom wasn't looking, he squirted some milk into his mouth. Tom always laughed at him for getting his fresh milk that way.

Mike and Tom were bringing the milk to the kitchen when Ma came to the door and called them to supper.

Martha had spread the best linen tablecloth and set out the best dishes. The table was loaded with good things to eat. There were baked squash with butter trickling over it, mashed turnips in cream, roast venison, mashed potatoes, sour cream gravy, and other things. Mike licked his lips. Pa showed each one where to sit, and Mr. Downs sat next to Pa.

Mike didn't say anything during supper. Children weren't supposed to talk at the table when there was company, and besides, he was too busy eating. Pa and Mr. Downs talked about President Grant, the governor of California, something they called politics, the new railroads, and other interesting things that Mike had never heard of. Once in a while Pat talked, too, but then, Pat was almost grown up.

"I have a couple of newspapers in my pack," said Mr. Downs. "The *San Jose Mercury* and the *Santa Cruz Sentinel*. They aren't exactly up-to-date, but I thought maybe you'd like to have them."

"I would," said Pa. "We don't keep up much on the news here."

"I always carry a few papers when I go into the wilderness," said Mr. Downs. "The forest families don't often get new reading matter."

"No," said Pa. "But the forest is the place to live, even if a body can't keep up on the news of which country is fighting which. But I fear that someday the forests will be gone, and there will be no more wilderness to move to."

"I don't think so," said Mr. Downs. "I believe that our government will recognize the value of the forests and close some of them to logging."

"Do you really think so?" Pat asked.

"I do. Right here is one of the best of the stands of coast redwoods. I wouldn't be surprised if all this area would one day be a public park."

They sat and talked after the berry shortcake was gone. Mr. Downs wanted to hear about the tanbark business and the lumbering that was going on around Boulder. When it began to get dark, they went into the front room and built up the fire in the fireplace. Ma lit the special kerosene lamp as well as the candles, and Mike thought the room looked real pretty.

Ma shoved the trundle bed into the corner of the room and put Sean and Liam to bed. They were fast asleep before Mike could wink. Rosie's cradle was in the girls' room. Mary was sitting in the corner near the fire, holding her redwood doll. The others sat on chairs around the fire, and Mike stretched out on a thick braided rag rug. He watched Mary playing with the doll until she fell asleep and Pa carried her in to her bed.

The men talked about politics until after Mary was asleep. Then they talked about the forest again.

Mike was feeling drowsy. He couldn't understand much of the talk. Then Mr. Downs said something that made his ears prick up right away.

"Ever see any bears in the redwoods?" he asked Pa.

"No," Pa said. "There aren't any bears. They were all killed off years ago."

"The loggers thought they were all killed," said Mr. Downs. "About a week ago, though, one of the loggers was attacked by an old grizzly down near Boulder—"

"You don't say!" exclaimed Pa.

Mike sat up. A real bear in the forest!

"The man was killed," Mr. Downs went on. "Of course, the loggers don't always have guns with them, but fortunately this group did. One of the men shot at the bear and wounded it badly, but it got away."

"Takes more than one shot to kill a grizzly, I hear," said Pat.

"Yes," said Mr. Downs. "They've sent out hunting parties to locate the bear, but they haven't found it again. People in Boulder are worried now for fear it will come again."

Mike was trembling with excitement and fear. What if the bear came near the cabin or the garden? He knew well enough how to shoot the gun that hung on the wall, always loaded for use, but if one shot didn't kill a grizzly—

Pa looked thoughtful. "I guess we'll have to watch more carefully when we're out for bark, and—"

"Ma'll have to keep the little ones close to the cabin," added Pat. "Mike's the only one at home that knows how to shoot."

"Ma can handle the gun," said Pa. "I taught her that the first time we moved into the wilderness."

Ma smiled. Mike knew she didn't like to shoot, but she did know how.

"The grizzly was old," said Mr. Downs. "They think it

will try to break into some cabin to get easy food. Or, of course, it may have been hurt badly enough that it will die."

"In a way, that would be bad," said Pa. "No one would know what had become of it. A person couldn't feel easy if he was alone in the forest."

Mr. Downs laughed softly. "That's right. I slept with one eye open last night myself."

"Our cabin is tight," said Pa. "You won't need to worry tonight." He stood up and stretched. "Morning comes early. Better be trotting up the ladder to bed, boys."

The boys climbed the ladder to the loft. Mike took a quick look at his pet snake before Pat blew out the candle. He tried to think of all the wonderful things Mr. Downs had told him about the forest so that he wouldn't dream about grizzly bears sneaking around the cabin.

Chapter 15

Mike in Charge

Mr. Downs left soon after breakfast the next morning. Mike went a little way down the creek with him.

"Well, Mike," said Mr. Downs, "I'm glad I got to visit you. I hope you'll keep on watching the creatures in the forest. Then someday you will be a naturalist, too."

Mike stood on a rock in the middle of the creek and watched Mr. Downs go on downstream. He wished Mr. Downs would stay longer. There were so many things he wanted to ask him. Why, he was almost as good a friend to have as Jake was.

Mr. Downs turned toward him once more and waved. "Goodbye, Mike. When I go through Santa Cruz, I'll send you a package to help you learn to be a naturalist." He started on again and was soon out of sight past a bend in the creek.

Mike waded slowly upstream to the cabin again. Pa had said that no one was to go far from the cabin until the bear had been located.

"We may have eight children," Pa had said, "but we can't spare any of them." He had checked the gun, too, before he left for the day.

The next few days were busy ones. Martha went with Mike to harvest the rest of the vegetables—the cabbages for kraut, and the turnips, carrots, and beets. Mike took the gun with them, and they kept a watch for the grizzly.

Mike often wondered what would be in the package Mr. Downs had promised to send. He knew that he wouldn't find out before Pa made his next trip to Boulder, for that was as far as the package would be brought. But that wouldn't be long, for soon the fall rains would begin, and Pa wanted to have the bark in Santa Cruz by then.

One morning, early in October, after Mike finished his milking, the warmth of the house seemed especially welcome after the cold mist outside.

Mary was dancing a jig in the middle of the kitchen floor.

"Happy birthday, Mike," she sang, clapping her hands. "Come and see what you've got."

Mike set the milk pails down quickly on the bench, and as fast as a boy who had newly turned ten could walk with dignity, he followed Mary to the front room.

In the middle of the floor, Mike saw a small set of shelves and a chest, pink and shiny in the firelight.

"Aren't they beautiful?" Mary asked. "They're for all your shells and drawings and things. Pa and Pat and Tom made them for you."

Mike dropped to his knees to examine the little redwood chest. He ran his hand over the polished wood and felt the carved letters of his name on the lid. Best of all he liked the bright brass hinges and lock.

Pat and Tom were standing with their hands in their pockets watching him proudly. Pa and the two little boys

were sitting on the trundle bed, and Ma and Martha stood in the doorway.

"Here's the key, Mike," Pat said.

"Oh, thank you," said Mike. He didn't say so, but he knew that now his precious things would be safe from Sean. Too often Sean would sneak up the ladder to the loft and muss up his things, or try to draw in his copybook.

Tom patted the set of shelves. "I almost wish I could be ten again."

Everyone laughed. Mike knew that Tom wouldn't go back to being ten years old for anything. But he did hope that since he was ten, Pa would count him one of the big boys like Tom and Pat, and let him go along on the trips into the forest and to Boulder.

Since it was a special day, Ma had fixed corn fritters for breakfast, and Martha set down a big slab of the wild honeycomb Pa had found. Mike ate so much that he could hardly fasten his belt around him.

"Sure and you'd better save some room for your dinner, Mike," Ma said when he finished his fourteenth fritter. "You've eaten as much as Pat."

Mike grinned. "Maybe I'll grow as big as Pat."

"Don't be in a hurry," Pat said. "You've got several years to go yet."

A few mornings later, Pa said that he would start that day for Santa Cruz. Ma and Martha hurried around fixing some food for him and the older boys to take with them to eat on the way. Ma had already made a list of things Pa was to buy in Santa Cruz, because he wouldn't be making the trip again for a long while, maybe a year. During the winter and early spring, the roads would be too muddy for the wagon.

Pa had the log sled that he used for carrying the bark standing in front of the house. Mike helped Pat load the dried, twisted bark crosswise on the sled. It made a full load. Pat roped it on tightly.

"Don't want to lose any of this twisted brown gold," Pat puffed, as he tightened the ropes.

"Will the wagon be full?" Mike asked. He didn't know how much bark Pa had drying in Boulder.

"Sure," said Pat. "We'll have it loaded so high that it will take all three donkeys to pull it."

Pa came out to see if they had the sled ready.

"Pa, what do they use the bark for in the tannery?" Mike asked. He couldn't see any connection between bark and leather except that one was outside the tree and the other outside the cow.

"In the tannery they have huge kettles bigger than barrels. They put the bark and water in these like a big stew and cook it. The hot water takes a stuff called tannin out of the bark. Then they use this tannin broth to tan the leather."

"I see," said Mike. "And that's why we call the tree a tanbark oak—because it has tannin in the bark."

"That's right," said Pa.

Tom brought the donkeys and hitched two of them to the sled. The other one was carrying a load of corn to be ground into meal.

The whole family, even Rosie in Ma's arms, gathered on the front porch to see Pa and the boys leave. They had been gone overnight before to Boulder, but this time they would be away for at least a week. Besides, though no one mentioned it, Mike knew that everyone was thinking about that grizzly bear.

"Mike," said Pa as he took up the reins of the team, "I'm leaving you in charge. Be sure to keep the gun loaded—you know where the bullets are. And keep an eye on the little shavers. I don't want them wandering off into the forest."

Mike stretched himself up an extra inch. "Yes, sir, Pa. I'll keep my eye on things." He was happy that Pa trusted him to be the man of the house, even though he was disappointed not to be able to go to Santa Cruz.

Pa smiled and then waved at the three little ones and the baby. "Let's go, Pat," he called.

Pat started down the path with the first donkey. He had his gun over his shoulder, and to Mike he looked like a grown man. Pa said, "Giddap," and the team of donkeys slowly pulled the log sled with the load of bark. Tom walked on the other side from Pa. He carried an ax in case they had to clear any underbrush out of the sled's way. Soon they were out of sight in the redwoods.

Chapter 16
Grizzly!

Mike felt a bit lonesome when he woke up in the loft and couldn't hear Pat snoring or Tom moving in his sleep. Then he remembered that Pa had left him as the man of the house. He jumped out of bed quickly and dressed by the gray light from the loft window. The mist drifting in through the window made him shiver. He hurried down the ladder to the warm front room and then out through the kitchen, where Ma and Martha were already busy.

When he had finished the milking, Martha had the table set for breakfast.

"Since you're taking Pa's place," she teased, "you may as well sit here at the head of the table."

Mike laughed and sat down quickly on Pa's sturdy bench. "I'll have a big bowl of mush and six eggs," he said in a deep voice.

"So," said Martha, "who do you think you are? The hens only laid five eggs yesterday—they're moulting, you know. You can only have one egg, Mr. Mike O'Grady."

After breakfast Mike took the ax and the gun and set off for firewood. He would have to cut plenty of firewood to be ready for the rainy weather. The first trees Pa had chopped down were dry enough to cut fairly well now. Since he wouldn't be going far, he let Sean and Liam tag along.

Mike could feel his muscles bulge when he chopped the tough wood. At this rate, he would soon be as strong as Tom. Anyway, he hoped so. Sean and Liam played in the leaves and collected acorns and acorn cups to play with. Before long they had all their pockets bulging with the acorns and tiny redwood cones. Mike always marveled that the immense redwood trees should have such small cones.

At noon they heard Martha calling, so Mike stuck the ax into the log, and they trooped back to the house for dinner. All afternoon Mike chopped wood, and by suppertime he had quite a pile cut. After Pa came back from Santa Cruz, they would haul the wood to the house on the sled.

Again the next day Mike chopped wood. Sean and Liam had tagged along, so he was careful to see that they stayed close by him. He wasn't going to let them wander away and get chased by a bear. He kept the loaded gun near him on a stump.

He was glad when he heard the call to supper, and they could return to the cabin.

After supper Ma needed a bucket of water. By the time Mike had finished the milking, the sky was murky dark with mist. He fed the calf and put Maury and Bossy in their stalls.

The mist became lighter, and Mike knew the moon had come up. He could make out the shapes of the trees and the woodshed. He saw a deer cut across the yard and then streak away into the night.

He made sure the chickens were all in and then fastened the door of the cowshed securely for the night. Picking up the two pails of milk, Mike started toward the house.

Suddenly his heart stood still! He saw the black hulk of an animal shuffling toward him out of the forest. He couldn't make out its shape, but it looked as big as two cows.

He knew it must be the grizzly bear. Had it seen him yet? Would it try to race him to the house? He didn't have the gun. What could he do?

Without waiting to think, he dashed for the kitchen door. Milk splashed out of the pails as he kicked the door open.

Ma looked at him in astonishment as he stumbled in. "What—" she began.

"The grizzly," Mike said. He bolted the door and stood inside trembling from his fright.

Ma went calmly through the rooms to see that all the shutters were bolted tightly, and Martha checked the bolts on the other two doors.

Mary began to cry, and Sean and Liam were wide-eyed with fear.

"Hush," said Mike. "The bear can't get inside the house." He was glad he had shut up the cows before the bear came. If he hadn't, there might not be any cows by morning.

Ma put the three little ones to bed, but they were too frightened to go to sleep. Finally Ma sat beside the trundle bed and sang all the old Irish lullabies she knew until Sean's and Liam's tired eyes drooped shut. Mary had already cried herself to sleep.

Mike walked slowly through the rooms listening to the bear sniff around the house. He wondered if the shutters would hold if the bear really tried to get inside. The grizzly spent most of his time sniffing around the outside of the kitchen and pantry. He seemed to smell the food.

Martha and Ma went about their kitchen work as if the sniffing came from a deer. But Mike knew they were frightened, too. He wished he could do something. How long would the bear stay? Would he keep them shut up in the house for the next five or six days until Pa came back from Santa Cruz? Mike knew he would have to get to the cows before then, for they would have to be fed and milked and watered.

Finally he went up the ladder to the loft. He peered out the window through the mist, bright now with moonlight. Below him was the bear. He shuddered to see how immense it was. He had never dreamed that even grizzly bears were so big!

But seeing the bear below him gave him an idea. He went downstairs and got the gun and extra bullets. Up in the loft again, he checked the gun to be sure it was ready to shoot, and then put the extra bullets into his pocket. He looked out the window, but the bear had gone around the corner of the house.

Mike thought of a daring plan. If it worked, fine. If it didn't—well, he just wouldn't think of that. He couldn't fail. Pa had left him in charge; he wasn't going to let that bear hurt Ma or Martha or the little ones.

He stood up in the loft window, facing the house, and looked across the roof. He had climbed onto the roof once before this way. He was sure he could do it again. Carefully he placed the gun on the roof so it wouldn't slide away. Then he pulled himself cautiously over the edge of the eaves and drew his legs up. Safe on top, he stopped a minute to catch his breath. He was outside with the bear now, and he hoped the bear wasn't tall enough to climb onto the roof of the lean-to.

Quietly he crept down the slope of the roof to the edge. He'd have to be close when he shot the bear. He could hear it sniffing along the kitchen wall, slapping at the boards with its paw and shaking the shutters.

Mike sprawled out on his stomach and readied the gun toward the place where he could hear the bear. He was almost on the edge of the roof, but he didn't dare lean over. When he was ready, he took a deep breath. Could he do it now?

He took another deep breath. Why didn't the bear hear his heart pounding and look up?

He whistled sharply.

The bear rose to his hind feet to see where the noise came from. Mike shot.

With a roar, the bear crashed against the house. Mike trembled as he reloaded the gun in the dim light. The bear had been so tall standing on its hind legs that it could have stretched out and cuffed him!

He got to his knees and looked cautiously over the edge of the roof. The bear was trying to rise. Mike aimed again and fired. The bear quivered and lay still.

But Mike wasn't taking any chances. He fired twice more.

He could hear Ma and Martha running across the loft to the window.

"Mike, Mike!" Ma called. "Are you all right?"

Mike watched the bear for a few minutes to be sure it was dead. Then he walked up the roof to the ridge. "I'm alright, Ma," he said softly. "Here, take the gun." He held it over the edge of the eaves and Ma took it. Then he lowered himself feet first, and Ma and Martha helped him through the window.

He staggered to his bed and flopped down on it, exhausted.

"Ma," he said. "I was never so scared in my life! The bear was as big as—as—as a redwood tree!" He buried his face in his hands and sobbed.

Ma patted him on the shoulder. "There, there, Mike. Every brave person is afraid. A person is brave because he does what he should, even when he is scared."

Mike looked up at her. "Do you really mean that, Ma?"

"That's right, Mike. If a man isn't afraid, he really isn't being brave at all."

Mike smiled now.

"Come down to the kitchen and have a hot drink," Ma said softly. "You're cold."

Mike followed her willingly down to the warm kitchen. She heated some milk at the fireplace in the front room, and Martha put it into Pa's coffee mug with a big chunk of butter that soon melted into golden bubbles. Mike sat at the kitchen table sipping it.

"We'll see about the bear in the morning," Ma said. "Nobody will bother it during the night."

Mike agreed. After he finished the hot milk, he climbed to the loft and in a few minutes was sound asleep, dreaming about shooting grizzly bears as big as redwood trees.

It was barely daylight the next morning when Mike ran quietly down the ladder and outside into the mist to take a close-up look at the bear. In the dim light, it looked like a huge black rock against the house. Mike was proud that he had been able to save the family from harm by killing it.

After breakfast was over and the morning chores were done, Ma and Martha came out with sharp knives and began to skin the bear.

"It was old," Martha said, "but we'll still have a fair rug for the front room."

"And plenty of bear steak," said Ma. "Though I'm afraid it'll be tough."

"He has lots of scars," said Mike. "He's been shot at before."

The little children had been watching without a word, but now Mary shuddered. "I'm glad Mike shot that big old bear before he got into the cabin." She began to cry.

"Don't cry now, silly," Mike said. "He can't hurt anyone again."

Mary began to laugh through her tears. "I was so scared last night that I cried, and now I had to cry because I'm so glad it's dead."

Mike shook his head. Sometimes it was hard to figure out why Mary did things.

Mike fixed a framework with poles, and they stretched the bearskin to dry.

"Let's put it where Pa will see it the first thing," Mike said.

Martha laughed. "Now, Mike, you wouldn't want to show off a bit, would you?"

Mike grinned sheepishly. "Well, don't you think it would be kind of nice for him to know the bear is dead?"

"Sure, we'll put it right by the front porch," Ma said, smiling at Mike. And they did.

Mike could hardly wait for Pa and Pat and Tom to return. He put a mark on the kitchen door for each day they were gone. After a week had gone by, he stayed close to the cabin to do his wood-chopping. He didn't want to be away when they came.

Nine days after the three had left, Mike was piling wood into the shed when he heard a donkey bray. That would be their donkeys! Pa was early. Mike hadn't expected them to come until late afternoon, but it wasn't even the middle of the afternoon yet. They must have left Boulder way before daylight, or else camped out once.

Mike dropped the load of wood and ran to the cabin. He pushed open the back door. "I hear the donkeys," he yelled inside. Then he ran around the cabin and down the path toward the creek.

He heard the front door slam, and Mary running after him, and Sean and Liam wailing, "Wait, Mike, wait!"

He stopped and waited for the little boys, but Mary scampered right on ahead of him.

"I wanted to tell them," Mike thought bitterly. Then he smiled. Better to let Mary tell them about the bear. He was ten years old and shouldn't brag. And Ma had already said he was brave. He took the little boys by the hand and led them down the bank of the creek and on to meet Pa.

Then he saw them. Pa was ahead leading a donkey. Pat and Tom were guiding the team of two donkeys with the log sled. The sled was piled with bundles and bags. Mike could hardly wait to see what was in all of them.

Mary was dancing along beside Pa. Mike could hear her. "—and it's huge, Pa! It was the biggest bear I ever saw!"

Mike laughed to himself. Mary had never seen a bear before at all! He went shyly toward Pa. He wasn't quite sure what Pa would say about the bear. But Pa didn't say anything. He only grinned and said, "Hello."

Ma and Martha were waiting on the porch. Pa looked at the bearskin, and Pat and Tom whistled. But still Pa didn't mention the bear.

Pat and Tom began to unload the bundles. "Here's the cornmeal, and a couple of sacks of flour," Pat said, lifting them to the porch.

"And the cloth and thread and buttons and other things you wanted, Ma," Tom said.

Pa took the cloth covering off the mysterious, bulging object in the middle of the sled.

"The stove!" Ma exclaimed. "How wonderful!"

Mike looked at her quickly. She looked as happy as Mary had with her little redwood doll or Sean and Liam with their boats. That reminded him of something. Had Mr. Downs sent the package?

Pa unloaded the rest of their winter supplies. Then he handed a medium-sized package to Mike. On the outside was his name—Mike O'Grady from Hiram Downs.

Mike tore off the wrapper eagerly. Several things! He sat down on the edge of the porch to look at each. The rest of the family crowded around.

"Two books!" said Tom. "Aren't you the lucky one?" He picked them up. "*Western Trees and Plants* and *Animals and Birds of the West*! And what beautiful pictures!" He sat down beside Mike to examine them more carefully.

"And a drawing book, too," Mike said, opening the tablet. "With no spelling or writing in the middle of the pages."

"Colored pencils," Mary said, picking up a package that had slipped off his lap. "They're just like the ones Mr. Downs had."

Mike grinned. "Now I can begin to be a real naturalist."

Ma and Martha turned to the shiny black-and-nickel pot-bellied stove again. Ma opened the oven door and peeked in at the shiny grates.

Mary and the little boys began to open the bundle of cloth and sewing things. Liam tried to count the buttons on the cards. "One, two, three, ten, eleven, twenty!" he said.

Mary laughed and hugged him. "Someday you'll learn to count straight!"

Mike was looking over Tom's shoulder at the pictures in the precious new books. Then he noticed that Pa was examining the bearskin. He walked over and stood beside him.

His father turned and put his hand on Mike's shoulder. "Well, Mike, I'm proud of you."

Mike's heart jumped. Pa had called him Mike! Was he really going to be one of the big boys now, and not just the middle one?

Pa was speaking again. "Pat has decided to work at the new mill that's starting up in Boulder. I'll be needing another hand on the tanbark in the spring, Mike. Do you suppose—"

Mike's eyes were shining. "Oh, Pa, let me help you! I'm ten years old now—"

"And brave enough to shoot a grizzly bear." Pa's eyes twinkled. He put out his rough, calloused hand and solemnly shook hands with Mike. "It's agreed then. Next spring you'll take Pat's place."

And now Mike knew that he was really a redwood pioneer.

MORE BOOKS FROM THE GOOD AND THE BEAUTIFUL LIBRARY!

His Indian Brother
by Hazel Wilson

The Mail Wagon Mystery
by May Justus

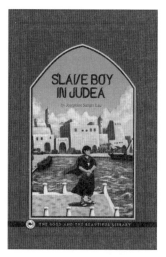

Slave Boy in Judea
by Josephine Sanger Lau

Juddie
by Florence Wightman Rowland

WWW.THEGOODANDTHEBEAUTIFUL.COM